WHO IS THE GREATEST OF ALL TIME?

For our England football heroes
M.O. & S.B.

Remember, our footballers are still playing and scoring goals. All stats in this book are up to 31 May 2025.

First published 2025 by Walker Books Ltd
87 Vauxhall Walk, London SE11 5HJ

2 4 6 8 10 9 7 5 3 1

EU Authorized Representative: HackettFlynn Ltd, 36 Cloch Choirneal, Balrothery, Co. Dublin, K32 C942, Ireland. EU@walkerpublishinggroup.com

This book has been typeset in ITC Giovanni

Printed and bound in Australia by Griffin Press

British Library Cataloguing in Publication Data: a catalogue record for this book is available from the British Library

ISBN 978-1-5295-3098-8

www.walker.co.uk

THE FOOTBALL GOAT

INDEPENDENT & UNOFFICIAL

KANE v. BELLINGHAM

MATT OLDFIELD

SETH BURKETT

WALKER BOOKS

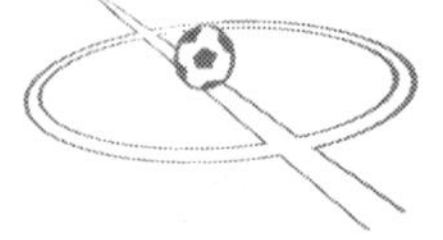

CONTENTS

HALF-TIME

STATS

CONTRIBUTION

EXTRA TIME

OTBALL GOAT KANE V

GHAM THE FOOTBALL

KANE V. BELLINGHAM

OTBALL GOAT KANE V

GHAM THE FOOTBALL

KANE V. BELLINGHAM

OTBALL GOAT KANE V

GHAM THE FOOTBALL

KANE V. BELLINGHAM

OTBALL GOAT KANE V

GHAM THE FOOTBALL

KANE V. BELLINGHAM

OTBALL GOAT KANE V

GHAM THE FOOTBALL

KANE V. BELLINGHAM

OTBALL GOAT KANE V

GHAM THE FOOTBALL

KICK-OFF

WHAT *IS* A FOOTBALL GOAT?

Matt

Seth

Hi there, Matt and Seth here. We're two friends who love football. We're bringing you another epic Football GOAT battle, packed with amazing facts, sizzling stats and incredible stories.

Matt
And arguing. We didn't mention arguing.

Seth
Oh yeah, how could we forget that? It's my favourite part!

Matt
Hey, it's MY favourite part!

Seth
Fine, it's OUR favourite part. Happy?

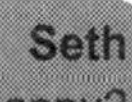

Matt
Not until this GOAT battle is over and won … by me!

In this football hero head-to-head, we're going all "Three Lions on a Shirt" for an exciting England debate.

Bobby Moore, David Beckham, Wayne Rooney – over the last 150-plus years, so many world-class players have worn the national team shirt with pride. But we're not here to pat them all on the back. We're here to vote for a current superstar who is one of the England team's…

GREATEST OF ALL TIME.

We're pitting two present-day England players against each other:

- The experienced number 9 v. the exciting young number 10…
- The current captain v. the future captain…

IT'S KANE V. BELLINGHAM!

NAME	Harry Kane
DATE OF BIRTH	28 July 1993
BIRTHPLACE	Walthamstow, London
POSITION	Striker
SHIRT NUMBER (CURRENT)	9
CLUBS	Tottenham Hotspur (2010–23) Leyton Orient (loan, 2011) Millwall (loan, 2012) Norwich City (loan, 2012–13) Leicester City (loan, 2013) Bayern Munich (2023–present)

NAME	Jude Bellingham
DATE OF BIRTH	29 June 2003
BIRTHPLACE	Stourbridge, West Midlands
POSITION	Central Midfielder/ Attacking Midfielder
SHIRT NUMBER (CURRENT)	10 for England 5 for Real Madrid
CLUBS	Birmingham City (2019–20) Borussia Dortmund (2020–23) Real Madrid (2023–present)

So, come on then ... who is the current leader of the Three Lions pack?

Matt
Let me guess. You think it's Kane, the guy who's never scored a big-game goal in his life.

Seth
No, let *me* guess! You're picking the wonderkid with attitude over England's top male scorer EVER.

Matt
Hmmm, maybe we should just go our separate, Football GOAT ways.

Seth
OR we could both present our best cases like we're in a football court, and then let the judge reader decide? That is kind of the aim of this book, after all.

Matt
OK, fine, but I hope you love losing as much as Kane does...

Don't worry, we're not the only ones who disagree about the England GOAT. This book will help you make up your mind in this tricky football debate. We're going to compare Kane and Bellingham – judging them head-to-head on a range of different qualities. Let's take a closer look at the categories:

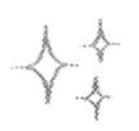

WHAT MAKES A FOOTBALL GOAT?

THEIR CHARACTER
We'll look at the mental side of the game: personality, mindset and leadership.

THEIR SKILLS
We'll study the full football skill set – physical, technical and tactical skills. And then we'll give you a half-time break.

THEIR STATS
Next up, we'll analyse the numbers – the goals and assists, the individual awards and the team trophies.

THEIR CONTRIBUTION
We'll end by looking at the bigger picture – how our GOATs have transformed their clubs, their countries and the beautiful game itself!

Sounds like a fair football fight, right? But before we let the battle begin, it's time to learn about the early lives and careers of our England GOATs…

ORIGIN STORIES: HARRY KANE

Harry was born just five miles away from White Hart Lane, the home of North London club Tottenham Hotspur. He grew up going to watch games there with his dad and brother, and dreaming of one day becoming a club legend, like his hero Teddy Sheringham. Harry's first taste of playing for a top football academy, however, actually came at Tottenham Hotspur's biggest rivals, Arsenal!

But aged nine, Harry was released after only one year, and when trials at Tottenham Hotspur and Watford didn't work out, he must have wondered if he would ever make it as a professional footballer.

DID YOU KNOW? Harry was born in the same hospital, went to the same secondary school (Chingford Foundation School) and played for the same local football club (Ridgeway Rovers) as former England captain David Beckham. Aged 11, Harry also trained with Becks at his new David Beckham Academy!

Eventually, the Tottenham Hotspur academy gave Harry a second chance, and playing in midfield, he successfully showed that while he wasn't the strongest or the fastest (yet!), he was definitely the most determined and dedicated. The coaches loved his attitude, and by the time he turned 17, they loved his first touch and fantastic finishing, too.

But instead of moving Harry straight into the first team, Tottenham Hotspur decided to send him out on a series of testing loans at lower-league teams.

First, in 2011, he went to Leyton Orient in League One, where he scored five goals and showed real bravery against big defenders.

Then, in 2012, he went to Millwall in the Championship, where his nine goals saved the club from relegation and won him their Young

Player of the Year award, despite only playing half the season!

It was so far so good for Harry, the loan ranger, but the next season didn't go so well. He struggled with injuries at Norwich City, and then he struggled for game-time at Leicester City. Nooooo!

When he returned to Tottenham Hotspur for the 2013–14 season, it felt like it was now or never to prove himself at his boyhood club.

During the first few months, Harry only played six games, but in December, Harry's old Tottenham Hotspur Under-21s coach, Tim Sherwood, became the new first-team manager. Surely he would get more game-time now?

Finally, in April 2014, Harry got his chance to start in the Premier League against Sunderland. And what happened next? He scored! Then he scored in the next game against West Brom, and again in the next against Fulham, too. Three goals in three games – Tottenham Hotspur had found their new star striker!

DID YOU KNOW? Harry never wore the number 9 shirt for Spurs. Instead, he started out wearing 37 (which he also wore at Millwall, Norwich and Leicester) before switching to 18 and then to 10.

Could Harry keep calm and keep scoring during the 2014–15 season? Oh yes, he fired in 31 goals for Tottenham Hotspur, plus five in five games for the England Under-21s. And it wasn't long before the England senior team came calling…

KANE'S BREAKTHROUGH MOMENT

ENGLAND 4 | 0 LITHUANIA

27 MARCH 2015 • WEMBLEY, LONDON

England were winning comfortably at Wembley in the qualifiers for Euro 2016, when manager Roy Hodgson decided to give an international debut to Tottenham Hotspur's new striking sensation, Harry Kane.

He came on for captain Wayne Rooney in the 71st minute and, within seconds, Kane had placed himself in the right place at the right time to head home Raheem Sterling's cross. GOAL! He had scored on his international debut! ■

Three days later, Kane started his first game for England, and the rest is football history…

KANE'S CAREER TIMELINE

– 2016 Harry scores 25 league goals for Tottenham Hotspur to win the first of his three Premier League Golden Boots.

– 2017 Despite his best efforts, Tottenham Hotspur finish as runners-up in the Premier League behind Chelsea.

– 2018 As the new England captain, Kane leads his country to the semi-finals in his first World Cup, and finishes as the tournament's top scorer with six goals.

– 2019 Harry helps fire Tottenham Hotspur to the Champions League final, where they lose to Liverpool.

– 2021 His England team reach the final of Euro 2020 (delayed due to Covid-19), but then lose to Italy on penalties.

– 2022 At the World Cup, Kane scores one penalty but then misses the second as England lose to France in the quarter-finals.

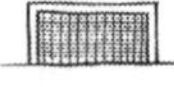

– 2023 Harry becomes the all-time record goalscorer for both Tottenham Hotspur (269 goals) and the men's England team (54). Then in August, after 19 years at Tottenham Hotspur, he leaves to sign for German giants Bayern Munich.

– 2024 After scoring 36 goals in the Bundesliga, the German top league, Kane wins his first-ever European Golden Shoe award in his first season at Bayern Munich. He also leads England to the Euros final again, where they lose to Spain.

– 2025 Harry is the top scorer in Germany again with 24 league goals, but most importantly, he wins the Bundesliga title with Bayern Munich, his first team trophy at last!

– 2026 Kane to play in his third World Cup.

ORIGIN STORIES: JUDE BELLINGHAM

Jude grew up in the West Midlands, watching his dad, Mark, banging in goals for their local non-league club, Stourbridge. At first, he didn't show much interest in football. But when he turned six, Jude caught the football bug big-time and began playing whenever and wherever he could.

DID YOU KNOW? Jude helped his primary school reach the national finals in both football AND cricket!

Like his England heroes Steven Gerrard and Wayne Rooney, Jude loved doing everything on a football pitch: passing, tackling, dribbling, shooting, even heading. And the more he practised, the better he became, until, aged seven, he was signed up by the Birmingham City academy.

Jude shone so brightly that the coaches had to keep finding new ways to challenge him. At first, they put him on teams with fewer or weaker players, but when that no longer worked, they just moved him up to older age groups.

- At 13, Jude was playing for the Birmingham City Under-16s.
- At 14, he was playing for the Under-18s.
- At 15, he was playing for the Under-23s, as well as training with the Birmingham City first team!

At his very first session for the first team, he faked to shoot, sent the captain sliding in the wrong direction and then calmly scored! Birmingham City had a future superstar on their hands.

How long could they keep him? One sensational season. In August 2019, Jude became the club's youngest-ever senior player, aged 16 years and 38 days. Just 25 days later, he became their youngest-ever goalscorer, too. For the rest of the season, he fought hard to help Birmingham City stay in the Championship.

DID YOU KNOW? In January 2022, Jude's record for being Birmingham City's youngest-ever senior player was nearly beaten ... by his own younger brother! Jobe Bellingham, who is also a midfielder, was just 69 days older when he made his first-team debut for the club, aged 16 years and 107 days.

So, what next for the boy wonder? Manchester United were desperate to sign Jude during the summer of 2020, but in the end, he decided to join German club Borussia Dortmund instead. His transfer fee was £25 million, making him the world's most expensive 17-year-old footballer ever!

Ousmane Dembélé, Jadon Sancho, Erling Haaland – Borussia Dortmund were famous for giving their young players lots of game-time in the German top league, the Bundesliga. But before he could make his debut for his new club, he had another debut to make for his country...

BELLINGHAM'S BREAKTHROUGH MOMENT

KOSOVO UNDER-21S	0 | 6	ENGLAND UNDER-21S

4 SEPTEMBER 2020
FADIL VOKRRI STADIUM, PRISTINA

The Under-21s Lions were winning comfortably in the qualifiers for Euro 2022 when manager Aidy Boothroyd decided to let 17-year-old midfield maestro Jude Bellingham make his international debut.

As he ran on in the 62nd minute, he became the youngest player ever to play for the Under-21s, but Bellingham was far from new to the international scene. No, he had already captained the England Under-15s, 16s and 17s!

So, could he now shine for the Under-21s, too? Yes! Bellingham quickly showed off the full range of his talent: his tackling skills to win the ball back on the edge of the Kosovo box, then his dribbling skills to cut inside on his right foot, and finally, his finishing skills to curl a shot into the bottom corner. GOAL! ■

Wow, there was just no stopping Bellingham now! Surely he was ready to play for the senior England team? The rest is football history…

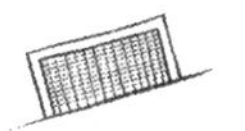

BELLINGHAM'S CAREER TIMELINE

– 2020 Two months after his Under-21s debut, Jude makes his senior England debut against the Republic of Ireland, still aged 17.

– 2021 Bellingham wins the German Cup with Borussia Dortmund.

– 2021 Jude is selected in the England squad for Euro 2020 (delayed due to Covid-19). He makes three super-sub appearances as the Three Lions reach the final, but then lose to Italy on penalties.

– 2022 At the World Cup, Bellingham starts every match in midfield for England, grabbing a goal and an assist.

– 2023 Despite Jude being named Bundesliga Player of the Season, Borussia Dortmund lose the league title to Bayern Munich on the last day of the season.

– 2023 Jude joins Real Madrid for £88 million and, playing in a more attacking role, he scores ten goals in his first ten games.

– 2024 Bellingham wins a trophy treble with Real Madrid: the Spanish Super Cup, La Liga (the Spanish league) and the Champions League. He's also named La Liga Player of the Season.

– 2024 Jude scores two goals in the Euros, including an incredible late overhead kick, as England make it through to the final. They lose to Spain.

– 2025 In his second season at Real Madrid, Jude wins two more trophies – the UEFA Super Cup and the FIFA Intercontinental Cup – but their Champions League and La Liga campaigns end in disappointment.

– 2026 Bellingham to play in his second World Cup.

So, those are the early life stories of our two England football GOATs – from boys with big dreams to superstars who made those dreams come true. That's enough football fairy tales, though. Now it's time to get ARGUMENTATIVE!

Here's a quick reminder of the two rules:

- It's fine to disagree, but NO dirty tactics.
- We use facts, but NO fake news.

Seth
OK, here's a fact to kick things off: there's no way Bellingham can be the GOAT because even I pocketed him.

Matt
Let's unpick that "fact", shall we? You can't pocket someone if you draw 1–1 against their team. And you were playing against MARK Bellingham … Jude's dad.

Seth
Hey, they share genes.

Matt
I feel sorry for the people you share genes with – there's a genuine fact for you. Now, where were we? Oh yeah, arguing about England's greatest-ever player…

But before the battle commences, we need to make clear just how BIG a deal it is to play for England.

ENGLAND – EVERY KID'S DREAM

"It's hard to put into words what it feels like to make your debut for England... It's what you dream about as a kid."

HARRY KANE

"International is the pinnacle of football."

JUDE BELLINGHAM

Football has the power to bring countries together to share in the joy or heartbreak of their national team. When England play in the Euros or World Cup, the country proudly watches, ready to celebrate every goal. And the biggest deal of all? Being England captain…

CAPTAIN FANTASTIC

There have been 128 male England football captains. Two early GOATs showed just how important the armband could be...

In 1959, Billy Wright was the first England player to receive 100 international caps. He captained England 90 times with his legendary leadership.

When Bobby Moore picked up the armband just a few years later, he continued that tradition. During his career he also captained England 90 times, but he did something that no other England captain has ever done … lift the World Cup!

THE 1966 WORLD CUP

In 1966, England hosted the World Cup for the first (and so far only) time. In front of a roaring home crowd, Alf Ramsey's Three Lions kept calm and went all the way, beating West Germany in the final 4–2 in extra time, thanks to a hat-trick from Geoff Hurst.

"They think it's all over … it is now!" went Kenneth Wolstenholme's famous BBC TV commentary. England had won their first-ever World Cup, and up walked Captain Bobby to collect the trophy from Queen Elizabeth and lift it high into the Wembley sky.

YEARS AND YEARS OF HURT

The 1966 World Cup win is still England men's only major international trophy (the Lionesses won Euro 2022 and 2025). Despite great expectations – and great leaders – England have experienced more pain than glory since that incredible World Cup.

ENGLAND PERFORMANCES (1968–PRESENT)

	WORLD CUP	EUROS
DID NOT QUALIFY	1974 1978 1994	1972 1976 1984 2008
DID NOT MAKE IT PAST THE GROUP STAGE	1982 2014	1980 1988 1992 2000
EARLY KNOCK-OUT DEFEAT	1998 (v. Argentina in the round of 16, on penalties) 2010 (v. Germany in the round of 16)	2016 (v. Iceland in the round of 16)
KNOCKED OUT IN THE QUARTER-FINALS	1970 1986 2002 2006 2022	2004 2012
KNOCKED OUT IN THE SEMI-FINALS	1990 2018	1968 1996
DEFEATED IN THE FINAL		2020 2024

Some of those disappointments we'll put down to bad luck – Diego Maradona's Hand of God goal for Argentina in 1986, for example – but others came from moments of madness, like Wayne Rooney's red card against Portugal in 2006.

In 1996, Baddiel and Skinner sang that England had suffered 30 years of hurt since 1966. By the 2026 World Cup, it'll be 60 years of hurt...

A GLITTERING FUTURE?

There are two major reasons why England's future appears brighter: current captain Harry Kane and future captain Jude Bellingham. We'll be using special England Insight boxes throughout this book to explain how our duo are taking England into a new era.

ENGLAND INSIGHT: 2026 WORLD CUP

At the 2026 World Cup in Canada, Mexico and the USA, England are one of 48 countries competing for the trophy. Will the Three Lions be triumphant? We'll have to wait and see, along with the 5 billion-plus other people who'll be watching the tournament...

First, let's discover what makes these GOATs tick...

CHARACTER

WHAT IS CHARACTER?

Before we get on to Kane and Bellingham's talents on the pitch, we're going to start by taking a closer look at what they're like as people, both on and off the pitch.

Why is that important? Well, because character and skill go hand in hand, like bread and butter, like modern footballers and mini shinpads.

Think of it this way: you might be able to score worldie after worldie in your local park, but if you can't stay calm and confident under pressure, how are you going to score them in Champions League finals or Euro penalty shootouts, with millions watching?

In this section we're going to look at:

PERSONALITY
We'll look at how Kane and Bellingham got the best out of their different personalities.

MINDSET
We'll study their mindsets – ways of thinking – and how they've overcame challenges during their careers.

LEADERSHIP
We'll end by looking at how they lead and inspire the people around them.

PERSONALITY

When you first compare their personalities, Kane and Bellingham seem like complete opposites:

- While one prefers a private life, the other loves the limelight.
- While one is Captain Calm, the other shows real passion on the pitch.
- While one is a man of few words, the other is never afraid to speak up.

We'll leave you to work out which is which! But if we delve deeper, these two superstars are more similar than they first seem…

HARRY KANE

Considering he's one of the best footballers in the world and the captain of England, we really don't know that much about Kane. But we know he loves:

1. Other sports, especially golf and American football
2. Spending time at home with his wife and four kids
3. Walking his two Labrador dogs, Wilson and Brady

Hmmm, that doesn't sound like a very exciting lifestyle, does it?

WHAT THE DOUBTERS SAY

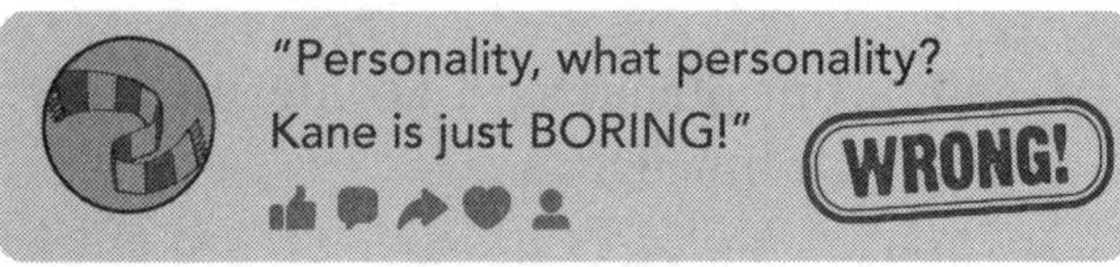

Close teammates talk about Kane's great sense of humour away from the TV cameras, but when it comes to football, he's always been the ultimate professional, putting performance first and personality second.

HE'S LOYAL

After his break-out season with Tottenham Hotspur in 2014–15, Kane could have signed for any of the world's biggest clubs and won lots of top team trophies. But instead he chose to stay at his local team, year after year, to try to win them a trophy.

When he did eventually ask to leave in 2021 and Tottenham Hotspur said no, Kane didn't throw a big tantrum. That season, he scored lots of goals, like always!

And when he finally left in 2023 to challenge for trophies, Kane chose to go to Germany and join Bayern Munich, rather than another English club. "I have made it clear my whole career that I am a Tottenham fan," he said.

For Kane, there's only one thing that comes before his club: his country. From making his senior England debut in 2015 to winning his 100th cap in 2024, he has hardly missed a match. Players who pull out of the less important international games because of club commitments? "I don't really like it, if I'm totally honest," Kane said.

> ***"England comes before club, it is the most important thing as a professional footballer."***
>
> HARRY KANE

HE'S DEDICATED

Of course, Kane has a talent for football (duh!), but it took him years of hard work to reach the top. Kane's old youth coaches all remember him as a player who was desperate to listen, learn and improve. "He was always the last player off the training pitch and the first onto it," said his England teammate Conor Coady back in 2015.

And ten years later, Kane hasn't changed at all. "Even now, he's still working as hard as a youth player who is trying to make it in the game," says his Bayern Munich boss, Vincent Kompany.

HE'S COMPOSED

Kane doesn't really do drama. When the pressure's on, he never lets it show, and when he scores a goal, he keeps his celebration short and simple.

"I am quite a calm character," Kane says. "I'm not someone who gets too irate or too low. I have a steady mind and I know my ambitions."

Kane helps keep those around him steady, too, especially younger teammates. But defenders should never underestimate England's Mr Nice Guy. He plays the game with the quiet confidence of a sniper, knowing that one shot is all he needs to score.

JUDE BELLINGHAM

As a young player, Kane was thought of as quiet and shy, but Bellingham? Never! This is a player in his early 20s who already has:

- His own showy goal celebration – standing in front of the fans with his arms out wide
- His own catchphrase – "Who else?"
- His own Adidas Euro 2024 advert

In fact, coaches, teammates and journalists often talk about the power of Bellingham's personality.

WHAT THE DOUBTERS SAY

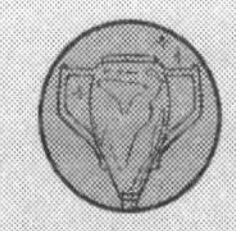

"Who does Bellingham think he is? He's so arrogant!"

WRONG!

HE'S CONFIDENT

Bellingham is a young player who really believes in himself, and what's wrong with that? You have to be confident to succeed at a club like Real Madrid!

If you're arrogant, you believe that you're already the best you can be, whereas Bellingham is always striving for more. "Jude listens and learns at the speed of light," says his old England Under-15s coach Kevin Betsy, while his former Real Madrid assistant manager Davide Ancelotti calls him "really receptive. He is so easy to coach."

Away from the football pitch, people describe a very different Bellingham, who remains as humble and polite as ever, and that's partly thanks to his parents. When he was a rising star at Birmingham City, Mark and Denise encouraged their son to take things step by step, in order to stay grounded. Even now that he's a Real Madrid superstar, his mum is still there, cooking for him and driving him to training most days!

"I get called arrogant a lot... I need to be confident because someone has to believe in me. Off the pitch I feel I'm a really normal guy."

JUDE BELLINGHAM

HE'S DRIVEN

To rise from Birmingham City to Real Madrid, one of the greatest clubs in the history of football, in just four years, you've got to have a fierce determination to succeed, right?

Bellingham plays every game with passion and energy, and he never stops until the final whistle. For him, there's only one feeling better than winning, and that's scoring the last-minute winner himself!

Bellingham always gives absolutely everything he's got, and he expects everyone around him to do the same. If they don't, he'll definitely let them know he's not impressed. "I'll never be satisfied," super-competitive Bellingham admits. "I always feel like I hate losing more than I enjoy winning."

HE'S MATURE

When Bellingham joined the Birmingham City first team as a 15-year-old, striker Lukas Jutkiewicz was amazed to see him "holding his own not just in training but in conversations". Two years later, former Manchester United manager Ole Gunnar Solskjær called Jude "the most mature 17-year-old I have ever met in my life".

But what exactly makes him seem older than his years? He carries himself – head high and confident – like he always has a plan, and it's also the way he communicates. In matches, Bellingham supports his teammates, and in interviews, he is honest and insightful. When he has something to say, he says it – and well!

He does have a passionate side, though, and his temper sometimes gets him into trouble, especially with referees. But we all need weaknesses to work on, don't we?

WHO'S THE WINNER?

Sorry, one personality doesn't beat another, even if you're as competitive as Bellingham. Our England football GOATs are both winners here!

And despite their other differences, Kane and Bellingham do share a relentless determination, which leads us neatly on to mindset…

MINDSET

Professional football superstar: dream job, eh? You get to play the game you love in front of thousands of adoring fans, while earning loads of money – EASY!

WRONG! Actually, there's a lot that can and does go wrong, even for top footballers like our England GOATs. Yes, Kane and Bellingham have both:

- Finished runners-up in title races
- Lost major finals
- Missed penalties
- Faced criticism for poor performances

Now, that list might sound terrible, but this is where a positive mindset can really save the day. Because what separates the good from the GOATs is how they react to setbacks: do they give up or give more? Do their heads drop or stay held high?

The answer: when the going gets tough, the GOATs keep going!

HOW TO BOUNCE BACK LIKE HARRY

"I believe Harry Kane is the best player in the world in terms of mental strength, willpower and endeavour."

MAURICIO POCHETTINO,
FORMER TOTTENHAM HOTSPUR MANAGER

Whether you agree or not, Kane has certainly shown remarkable resilience throughout his career for his clubs and country.

As a young player, he had to fight really hard to make the Tottenham Hotspur first team, proving himself again and again. Even during four different loans at four different clubs, Harry never gave up on his dream.

In fact, his breakthrough mindset moment actually came during one of those tough loan spells, aged 18, after watching a documentary about his NFL hero, Tom Brady. As a young player, Brady was told he wasn't good enough to be a star, but he proved everyone wrong by becoming one of the greatest quarterbacks ever.

Inspired by what he'd seen, Harry made a plan: "I just needed to do what he'd done: work harder, believe in myself more, and hopefully, one day, become one of the best." So that's exactly what he did. He was dedicated: spending hours in the gym getting stronger and out on the pitch improving his striking skills.

When Kane finally got his chance at Tottenham Hotspur in 2014, the goals soon flowed, but the trophies didn't. Tottenham Hotspur finished second in the Premier League in 2017 and then lost in the Champions League final against Liverpool in 2019 and in the EFL Cup final against Manchester City in 2021.

So close, so many times! But Kane didn't give up. He carried on scoring goal after goal, game after game, season after season, until he became his club's all-time record goalscorer in 2023.

And it's been a similar story for Kane with England. There have been highs, but also some indisputable lows:

- The embarrassment of losing to Iceland at Euro 2016
- The thrill of reaching the World Cup semi-finals in 2018

- The excitement of reaching the final of Euro 2020
- The shared pain of losing that final against Italy in a penalty shoot-out
- The personal pain of missing a penalty in the 2022 World Cup quarter-final
- The agony of losing another Euros final in 2024

Throughout it all, Kane has remained England's rock, still doing what he does best: scoring goal after goal, game after game, year after year, until he became his country's all-time record goalscorer in 2023.

ENGLAND INSIGHT: NUMBER 9S

At the 1966 World Cup, England's number 9 shirt was worn by midfielder Bobby Charlton. More recently, it has belonged to the team's star striker. In the 1990s, that was Alan Shearer (30 international goals in 63 games); in the 2000s, that was Wayne Rooney (53 in 120 – who also wore 10); and since 2016, that has been Harry Kane, whose current record stands at 71 in just 105 games. Never has an England Number 9 been so consistent at scoring goals.

HOW TO HANDLE PRESSURE LIKE JUDE

"Jude was perfectly equipped mentally and physically. That winner's attitude is the number one thing that Real Madrid recognize."

GRAHAM HUNTER, JOURNALIST

Bellingham has proven time and time again that he can handle the pressures of elite football.

When he burst onto the scene as a 16-year-old at Birmingham City, all of England's biggest clubs started chasing him. But Bellingham never lost his focus. His team had a relegation fight to win and, with his help, they succeeded.

When Bellingham signed for Borussia Dortmund in 2020, for £25 million, he became the world's most expensive 17-year-old footballer EVER, but he didn't let that bother him either.

In his first season, he was subbed off at half-time in his Champions League debut against Lazio, and then again in the German Cup final. But he kept learning. And just two years later, he became Borussia Dortmund's top scorer and the Bundesliga Player of the Year!

What about when he arrived at Real Madrid, the biggest team in the world, in 2023? He decided to focus on the positives: "To have this responsibility feels like a huge privilege to me."

Rather than letting the club's history weigh him down, Bellingham embraced it, even taking the legendary number 5 shirt, previously worn by French icon Zinedine Zidane. And what's the best way to deal with high expectations? By writing your own history!

In his first El Clásico match, away at Barcelona's Camp Nou, Jude scored both goals for Real Madrid: a long-range rocket, followed by a last-minute winner. And in the second, back at the Bernabéu? He scored a last-minute winner again! As Jude himself would say, "Who else?"

But HOW does Bellingham handle that big-game pressure so well? It's a combination of his natural winner's mindset and smart preparation.

Before each match, he spends time out on the field, alone, visualizing what's about to happen in his head. "I see the pitch, the grass, my playing position," he explains. "Thanks to that I go into matches without nerves and prepared for everything".

So, there you have it: the secret to a superstar mindset.

WHO'S THE WINNER?

The Comeback King meets the Prince of Pressure – *ooof*, it's too close to call! But before we start arguing about the overall Character GOAT, there's one final category we need to consider: leadership.

Do these England superstars support and inspire the players around them, and if so how?

LEADERSHIP

In football, what do you think of when you hear the word "leader"?

- The tough talker who rallies the team?
- The hard worker who fights for every ball?
- The hero who always saves the day?

There are lots of different ways to be a leader, but supporting and inspiring others is definitely a GOAT characteristic. The more united and motivated everyone is, the more likely it is that the team will win.

So what are our England GOATs like as leaders? On one side, we have Kane, the current captain, and on the other, Bellingham, tipped to be the next in line to the armband. Let the battle begin!

CAPTAIN KANE

"He has belief and high standards," the England manager Gareth Southgate explained when he announced Harry Kane as the new national captain for the 2018 World Cup, "and it is a great message for the team to have a captain who has shown that it is possible to be one of the best in the world over a consistent period of time".

But did Kane really have enough experience for the job? This would be his very first World Cup, and he didn't even wear the armband for Tottenham Hotspur. Plus, what about the passion and personality?

WHAT THE DOUBTERS SAY

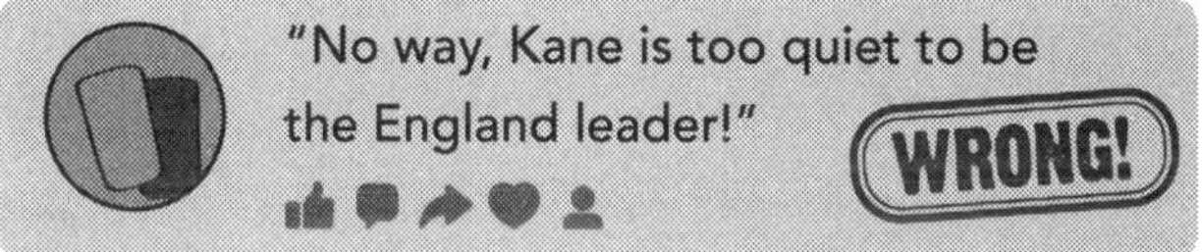

Harry would definitely be a different kind of captain from Wayne Rooney, Steven Gerrard and David Beckham before him – less loud and proud, more nice and ice-cool. But maybe that was what England's exciting new team, featuring the likes of Jordan Pickford, Harry Maguire and Dele Alli, needed. Because England were to face a penalty curse that had been unbroken for 28 years. With the nation holding its breath, was Captain Kane going to be the leader who finally broke it?

COLOMBIA 1 | 1 ENGLAND (4–3 ON PENALTIES)

3 JULY 2018 • OTKRITIE ARENA, MOSCOW

With seconds to go, it looked like Kane's cool spot-kick was about to send England through to the 2018 World Cup quarter-finals. But no, Colombia equalized, and the match went all the way to … PENALTIES!

Harry was determined to help end England's spot-kick curse, but how? With the pressure on, he did what he does best as a captain: bringing the players together and keeping everyone calm and confident, just like him.

Harry also believed in leading by example. So far in

PENALTIES

Since they were first introduced at Euro 1976, penalty shoot-outs had almost always ended in painful defeat for England:

TOURNAMENT AND ROUND	OPPONENTS	OUTCOME
1990 WORLD CUP, SEMI-FINAL	West Germany	Lost
EURO 1996, QUARTER-FINAL	Spain	Won
EURO 1996, SEMI-FINAL	Germany	Lost
1998 WORLD CUP, ROUND OF 16	Argentina	Lost
EURO 2004, QUARTER-FINAL	Portugal	Lost
2006 WORLD CUP, QUARTER-FINAL	Portugal	Lost
EURO 2012, QUARTER-FINAL	Italy	Lost

the tournament, he had already scored six goals, including the winner against Tunisia and a hat-trick against Panama.

But now, with the hopes and dreams of millions of fans weighing on his shoulders, Kane stepped forward first for his country, and … slammed an unstoppable shot into the bottom corner!

Not only had he scored, but he had shown the way for his teammates to follow. Eight spot-kicks later, England were celebrating their first-ever World Cup penalty shoot-out win!

"We stood up and were tall," Kane said, while back home, the country went wild. "It shows the togetherness and the character… I'm so proud of everyone." ■

England went on to reach the World Cup semi-finals for the first time since 1990, before losing to Croatia in extra-time. Although Kane was gutted, he didn't give up. "We can be proud and we'll be back," he declared, and the England captain kept his word.

Two years later, at Euro 2020, he led his team to another semi-final, and this time, they won, with Kane scoring the winner in extra-time! England went on to lose to Italy in the final, but even in defeat, Captain Kane led his team over to thank the fans for their support, uniting his country once again.

"We win together, we lose together."

HARRY KANE

One World Cup semi-final and two Euro finals – Kane has captained England in one of their most successful eras ever. And his calm, kind leadership style has been just as important to his team as his many, many goals.

BELLINGHAM THE BOSS

Bellingham's leadership skills were spotted at a very young age. As a 16-year-old, he captained the England Under-17s to Syrenka Cup glory, and by 19, he was already wearing the armband for Borussia Dortmund. And there's more to come. "If he stays here for a long time then he can be captain," his former Real Madrid manager Carlo Ancelotti has said. "And for England he will be."

Sure, Jude has the passion and drive for the job, but what about the composure?

WHAT THE DOUBTERS SAY

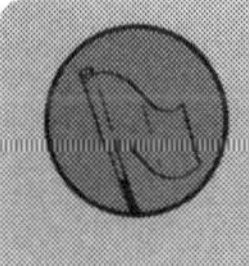

"Bellingham isn't calm enough to be England captain – he even gets angry with his own teammates!"

WRONG!

Bellingham does sometimes let his frustrations show, but most of his shouting on the pitch is positive, rather than negative. He sets high standards for himself and others, and he also supports his teammates in times of need, as he showed at the 2022 World Cup...

ENGLAND 1 | 2 FRANCE

10 DECEMBER 2022
AL BAYT STADIUM, AL KHOR, QATAR

When France went 2–1 up in the 2022 World Cup quarter-final, many England players threw their hands to their heads in despair. But not Jude Bellingham, their new main man in midfield.

With 15 minutes left, the 19-year-old was determined to make a difference for England. England were losing against France and it was Bellingham who led the fightback.

LINGHAM TS BACK

As journalist Jonathan Northcroft described it, "The youngest player on the team was trying to boss people. And trying to resist defeat the most…"

Bellingham kept pushing himself, until eventually his beautiful long pass led to a penalty for England.

Unfortunately, Harry Kane blasted it high over the bar, but who was the first teammate to put an arm around his shoulder? Young Bellingham, already displaying the qualities of a top leader. ■

Two years later, at Euro 2024, Jude joined England's four-man leadership group (along with Harry Kane, Kyle Walker and Declan Rice), playing a key part in taking the team all the way to the final with his endless energy and never-give-up attitude.

"Who else?" Jude shouted after saving the day with an unbelievable 95th-minute overhead bicycle kick in the round of 16 against Slovakia (more on this goal later). When it comes to choosing the next national captain, we expect most people will be saying the same thing.

WHO'S THE WINNER?

While Bellingham has definitely shown signs of becoming a great leader for his country, we're giving this one to Kane, who has proven over multiple tournaments that he has what it takes to captain England.

SO COME ON THEN... WHO IS THE CHARACTER GOAT?

In the Character section, we've looked at what our GOATs are like as people, players and leaders. But before you make your final decision, it's time for us to present our best arguments for both sides.

SETH'S CASE FOR KANE

Captain Kane doesn't need to shout about how amazing he is. Instead, he lets his feet do the talking. After all, why waste time boasting when you could be practising?

This ultra-dedicated pro isn't just a loyal and legendary leader. Thanks to his mega mindset, he stays strong through thick and thin.

His painful release from the Arsenal academy? Those lower-league loans? He never gave up and became captain of a Premier League club.

Those doubters who said he'd never be good enough? He became captain of his country.

But even though he wears the armband, it's never all about him. Kane is the ultimate team player, making the changing room a fun, friendly place.

Who would you prefer to have on your team: the humble hero or the loudmouth in midfield? Exactly…

MATT'S CASE FOR BELLINGHAM

England's Character GOAT? Easy!

It's … JUDE BELLINGHAM! The boy wonder from Birmingham City is a mentality monster: humble at home, but fearsome on the field.

- Confidence? *Tick!*
- Passion? *Tick!*
- Drive? *Tick!*

Performing under pressure? What pressure?! Whether he's playing for England or Real Madrid, Bellingham shines brightest in the biggest games, stepping up with last-minute moments of magic.

And whether he's sharing a pitch with Harry Kane or Harlee Dean (no offence!), Jude has shown that he's a natural leader, inspiring everyone around him with his relentless energy and determination to win.

So, of course Bellingham is the Character GOAT – I mean, come on, who else?

Seth
Erm, the actual England leader, who treats everyone with respect rather than shouting at them?

Matt
Oh, you mean the guy who always gets it wrong in the biggest games?

Seth
Hey, Kane scored the winner in the Euro 2020 semi-finals!

Matt
Oh sorry, I thought you were talking about Southgate.

Seth
Move on, mate – Gareth's gone! Thomas Tuchel's the manager now, and he's a winner.

Matt
Yeah, just like Jude.

THE SCORES ARE IN:

	KANE	BELLINGHAM
PERSONALITY RATING	8/10	8/10
MINDSET RATING	9/10	9/10
LEADERSHIP RATING	9/10	8/10
TOTAL SCORE	26/30	25/30

So that's what we think, but we're not the real decision-makers here – *you* are! Who do you think is the England Character GOAT and why?

My Character GOAT is

....

SKILLS

WHAT ARE SKILLS?

Out on the pitch, in front of thousands of fans, our Comeback King and Prince of Pressure love to show what they do best: their world-class skills!

Yes, we're talking about the plays that get fans off their seats in excitement. Think Kane's scintillating shooting, Bellingham's tenacious tackling … and everything else in between. Just like a box-crashing Bellingham or a hard-working Harry, we're going to cover a LOT of ground in this chapter.

But who is the GOAT with the most when it comes to skills? To work out that big question, we're going to break this chapter down into three key areas:

- **PHYSICAL SKILLS**
  We're talking speed, strength and power.
- **TECHNICAL SKILLS**
  We'll analyse Kane and Bellingham's technical skills – dribbling, passing and shooting.
- **TACTICAL SKILLS**
  Finally, we'll look at how our GOATs use tactical skills to influence their games.

PHYSICAL SKILLS

"Elite players are playing a more elite standard of football than ever. It's more physically demanding than ever."

JUDE BELLINGHAM

Top footballers have to play games at elite level week in, week out, over and over again. Each game is a minimum of 90 minutes and means:

- Sprinting into space
- Outmuscling opponents
- Jumping for headers
- Jockeying side-to-side
- Running more than 6 miles (10 kilometres) in EVERY SINGLE GAME!

That's no joke! We're getting tired just thinking about it, but thanks to their physical skills, Kane and Bellingham haven't just survived the high expectations. They've thrived! So how have they managed it?

HARRY KANE

Arsenal's academy dismissed him as "not very athletic". His Tottenham Hotspur academy coaches questioned whether he'd ever have the physicality to play professional football. England Under-21s manager Stuart Pearce said he lacked "that turn of pace". So when it comes to physical skills, Kane has spent much of his career proving people wrong…

HE'S … NOT ACTUALLY THAT SLOW!

OK, Harry isn't the fastest footballer who's ever played, but he's certainly no slouch! The average top speed of a professional footballer is around 19–20 miles per hour (31–32 kilometres per hour), which is already much faster than the average person on the street. Yet Harry Kane has hit a top speed of more than 20.5 miles per hour (33 kilometres per hour) several times in his career.

But he doesn't often need to use such speed. Instead, Kane ghosts into the half-space between defenders. Before defenders realize where Kane's gone, his magical movement has already given him a big head start!

HE'S SERIOUSLY STRONG

Those who claimed Kane wasn't physically mature were soon left eating their words. Kane carried on growing, eventually reaching a muscular 1.88 metres (6ft 2in) tall. "We've done a lot of work in the gym to work on my speed, on my fitness, on my strength … that's given me confidence … coming up against players now," he said back in 2015.

Under manager Mauricio Pochettino at Tottenham Hotspur, Kane became a serious physical force. Thanks to his hard work and physique, he could easily hold off defenders, ride challenges and win lots of headers.

HE NEVER STOPS

While many superstar strikers stay by the goal so they can wait to score, Kane's work ethic and loyalty mean he's always willing to work for his team. Thanks to his fantastic stamina, Kane covers lots of distance, racing back to defend and running forwards to create chances.

At Euro 2020, the 46.1 miles (74.3 kilometres) he ran was the fourth highest of all players at the tournament, and the second highest for England.

JUDE BELLINGHAM

Whether charging forwards, tracking back or outmuscling opponents, Bellingham has always been an all-action player. In part, that's thanks to his determination to never give up. But he's also helped by some impressive physical skills…

HE'S A WARRIOR

Standing at 1.86 metres (6ft 1in) tall, Bellingham is big. He uses his size in lots of clever ways – especially when throwing himself into battle. As a teenager in Birmingham City's first team, Bellingham wanted to show that he was "fearless and belong[ed] on the pitch". That meant getting stuck in!

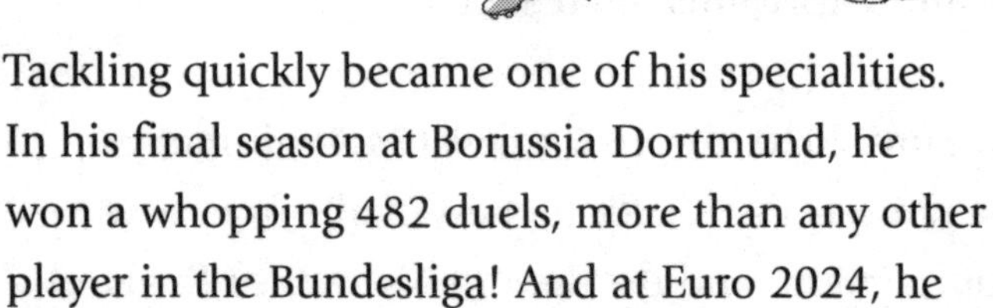

Tackling quickly became one of his specialities. In his final season at Borussia Dortmund, he won a whopping 482 duels, more than any other player in the Bundesliga! And at Euro 2024, he won 50 per cent more tackles than ANY other player in the entire tournament. As he says himself: "Every game's a war and you've got to be up for it."

HE'S RELENTLESS

As a box-to-box midfielder, Bellingham needs to score goals in attack AND prevent goals at the back. To cover so much ground, Bellingham does a LOT of running. At Euro 2024, Bellingham ran a ridiculous 47 miles (75 kilometres) across seven games – the third highest figure of all players in the tournament!

Bellingham's will to win and never-say-die attitude means he creates big moments late on in games. In his first 18 months at Real Madrid, Bellingham bagged six stoppage-time winners – the second highest number in Europe's top five leagues!

HE'S EXPLOSIVE

To get from one box to the other, Bellingham bursts past opponents with amazing acceleration. His long legs mean he has long stride length, plenty of power and a nippy top speed of 20.3 miles per hour (33.5 kilometres per hour). He leaves defenders in the dust!

WHO'S THE WINNER?

Hard-working Harry transformed his physical skills from *meh* to mega, but Bellingham is the ultimate warrior. Though they both have strength and stamina, we'd rather be on Bellingham's side in this battle. But what about technical ability?

TECHNICAL SKILLS

Once Kane and Bellingham have outmuscled, outsprinted or outleapt their opponent, they then have a decision to make: what to do with the ball? It's time to get technical…

ENGLAND INSIGHT: THE ENGLAND DNA

After poor performances at Euro 2008 and the 2010 World Cup, the English FA decided it needed a talent development overhaul. So they looked at how nine successful nations, like Belgium and Germany, taught their young players. The result was launched in 2014. The England DNA was England's official plan to create skilful players for the national team. The following year, Harry Kane made his England debut. And five years later another SUPER skilful player debuted … Jude Bellingham!

HARRY KANE

PASSING

When *FIFA*, the most popular video game in football history, announced its player ratings for the 2017 season, Kane was not happy. *FIFA* uses all the available data to award each player a rating out of 99. His passing had *only* been rated as 71. "It's better than 71!" he scoffed.

So what did Kane do? He proved people wrong. He demanded the ball and showed everyone his pinpoint passing range.

His Tottenham Hotspur manager was dazzled! "He has the skill to see the space in behind your defensive line," said Pochettino after yet another Kane assist. His England manager, Southgate, was also impressed: "He has got a fabulous weight of pass and great vision to see those passes."

The following season, *FIFA 2018* updated his passing to a rating of 93! By the 2020–21 season, Kane had won the Premier League's Playmaker award with 14 assists (he also won the Golden Boot that season, which is awarded to the player who scores the most league goals).

DRIBBLING

Unlike some other GOATs, you won't find many compilation videos of Kane doing awesome skills and beating loads of players. Why should he dribble past one or two players when he can take out a whole defence with one pass? Kane is all about efficiency – making the best decision for the team.

But that's not to say that Kane can't dribble. Towards the end of his Tottenham Hotspur career, he attempted 2.78 dribbles per game with a 54 per cent success rate – a similar success rate to demon dribbler Kylian Mbappé and far higher than Erling Haaland's 40 per cent.

SHOOTING

Shooting is our England hero's super power. Kane's perfect technique makes him just as deadly from outside the area as he is in it (he even scored from his own half in Bayern's 8–0 win over Darmstadt 98).

His shots are powerful. Against Stuttgart, his strike from 30 yards was recorded at 75.8 miles per hour (122 kilometres per hour). That's faster than a cheetah! They are also accurate. "He places the

ball with a precision and speed into the corners that goalkeepers just can't save," said Bayern Munich teammate Thomas Müller. "In terms of finishing – with both feet and his head – there is no one better."

DID YOU KNOW? *FIFA 18* gave Kane the maximum rating for his shooting skills: 99!

And Kane has the stats to prove it. In his first two seasons as a Bayern Munich player, nobody in Europe's top five leagues scored more goals per game than him!

	GAMES	GOALS	GOALS PER GAME
HARRY KANE	91	82	0.9
KYLIAN MBAPPÉ	104	87	0.84
ERLING HAALAND	89	69	0.78

Kane scores when others simply can't. In the 2016–17 season, data scientists worked out that he should have scored 19.82 goals (known as xG – expected goals), given the quality of his chances … yet he scored 29 goals!

Let's take a look at how other top finishers have outperformed their xG across their entire careers in Europe's top five leagues…

	DIFFERENCE BETWEEN XG AND GOALS
LIONEL MESSI	+33.11
HARRY KANE	+32.13
KYLIAN MBAPPÉ	+26.46
ERLING HAALAND	+9.11
CRISTIANO RONALDO	+4.54
JUDE BELLINGHAM	-2.03

When it comes to shooting, Kane isn't just world class. He's a GOAT.

JUDE BELLINGHAM

PASSING

Bellingham may have the physical skills of a warrior, but he has the technical skills of an artist. Thanks to an outstanding range of passing, Bellingham can go through, round or over defences. And he passes a lot – an average of 54 times per game for Real Madrid.

It's little surprise that Bellingham's teammates LOVE to give him the ball. Former Borussia Dortmund teammate Julian Brandt said: "You could always pass the ball to him. Under pressure or not, he didn't lose the ball."

DRIBBLING

With close control, speedy feet and smooth drops of the shoulder, Bellingham is like a dancer as he weaves through the tightest of opposition defences. Just look at his epic solo goal for Borussia Dortmund against Arminia Bielefeld in 2021 when he dribbled past three players before dinking the keeper.

In his final season at Borussia Dortmund, he completed 86 dribbles at a 57 per cent success rate – league-leading figures! In fact, between 2022 and 2024, no player in Europe's top five leagues bettered his dribbling success rate of 60 per cent!

SHOOTING

With over 70 career goals already, Bellingham's character and physical skills give him an edge in the area. His desire gets him to the ball ahead of defenders, and when he connects with a strike, his careful control gives him impressive accuracy. In his first season for Real Madrid, Bellingham scored one goal for every 2.7 shots he took!

"Inside the box I want to be a killer – someone the team can rely on to score goals in important moments."

JUDE BELLINGHAM

"He was always very good at finishing. He was more precise and didn't try to score with force. He was putting the ball into the corner."

ROMAN BÜRKI,
BORUSSIA DORTMUND GOALKEEPER

ALL-ROUND GAME

WHAT THE DOUBTERS SAY

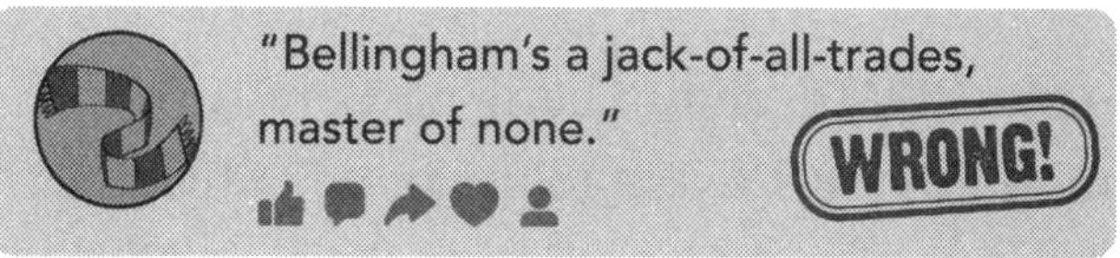

The beauty of Bellingham is his all-round game. Beyond passing, dribbling and shooting, this GOAT is ALSO a master at tackling, has no weak foot, and has such good control it's as if his boots are covered in superglue. "He has no weakness in his game," says England teammate Phil Foden.

Borussia Dortmund's reliable passer. Europe's best dribbler. Real Madrid's top scorer. And every single season he's improving: scoring more goals, making better passes and trying daring dribbles. "Jack" of all trades? More like "master"!

WHO'S THE WINNER?

Wow, this is a close one. These two GOATs can do everything. But while Bellingham is one of the best in the world in many areas, Kane IS the best in the world at finishing. Should he edge it? Maybe just... But does he have the football smarts to go with his finishing?

TACTICAL SKILLS

So our GOATs can run hard, pass precisely and finish for fun. But to use those individual physical and technical skills to the max, Kane and Bellingham need to power up their football brains.

They have to decide which skill to use at the right moment in a game. They need to fit their individual talents into the team's system … and they need to stick to their manager's gameplan. They need to have top tactical skills! But who do you think takes the crown?

HARRY KANE

WHAT THE DOUBTERS SAY

"For a striker, Kane spends way too much time in midfield."

WRONG!

Kane is a seriously clever footballer, and there's a reason he drops into midfield so often. As well as being a physically dominant number 9, he developed his game so that he could also play as a creative number 10 who makes and takes chances around the penalty area, or a fantastic false 9 who drops into midfield and ghosts into attack.

"In the game it's important to be able to adapt and see where you can hurt the opposition, whether that's dropping deep or staying high or being in the box for crosses," said Kane. "I let my instincts take over."

DID YOU KNOW? Harry's so versatile he's even played in goal! The less said about that the better though… He conceded a howler in Tottenham Hotspur's 5–1 Europa League victory over Asteras Tripoli in 2014.

"His capacity to understand the game is amazing," said his Tottenham Hotspur manager, Pochettino. "He senses what the team needs, and when it's under pressure he can drop into midfield to help the team progress the ball up the pitch or to provide assists."

Defenders may hate Kane's instincts, but his teammates love them. Especially one by the name of Son Heung-Min…

SOUTHAMPTON 2 | 5 TOTTENHAM HOTSPUR

20 SEPTEMBER 2020
ST MARY'S STADIUM, SOUTHAMPTON

In the changing room, Kane and Son went over the plan one final time: if Kane dropped deep into midfield, they were sure Southampton's defenders would follow him, leaving space for Son to charge in.

Now, they just had to go out and put their tactics into action…

Bosh! In first-half stoppage time, Kane's first-time pass found Son, who struck home. 1–1!

Boom! After 47 minutes, Kane's through ball sent Son to score his second. 2–1!

Bang! At 64 minutes, Kane dropped deep and played a ball over the top for Son's hat-trick. 3–1!

Bing! With 73 minutes gone Kane's cross-field pass found Son for his fourth goal of the game – and Kane's fourth assist! 4–1!

Woah, the pair had combined for four goals in just one game! And to add the icing on the cake, Kane scored Tottenham Hotspur's fifth goal after 82 minutes.

"I didn't even look for one [of the assists]," Kane said afterwards. "I just know he's running behind. We've been building the relationship." ■

And what a relationship it turned out to be! Kane and Son would go on to combine for 14 league goals in the 2020–21 season, and 47 league goals in total by the time Kane left Tottenham Hotspur: both Premier League records!

> ***"We created an almost telepathic connection with much more changing roles."***
>
> HARRY KANE

They were officially the deadliest duo to have ever graced England's top division … and it was all thanks to their brilliant tactical brains!

JUDE BELLINGHAM

Bellingham may now wear the number 5 shirt for Real Madrid and number 10 for England, but in his earlier years he wore 22. The reason? His tactical skills!

As a youngster in the Birmingham City academy, Bellingham told his coach Mike Dodds that he wanted to be an attacking midfielder: a number 10. "I think you can be a 22," Dodds replied. He meant that Bellingham could also be a number 4 (holding midfielder) and a number 8 (box-to-box midfielder). He was so good he could do it all!

Hmmm… Bellingham took some time to do the maths.

10 + 4 + 8 = 22

It all added up! So together with Dodds, he learned how to create like a number 10, to break up play and make tackles like a number 4, and impact both boxes like a number 8. Thanks to his physical and technical skills, he soon became three players in the body of one.

ENGLAND INSIGHT: MIDFIELD MANIA

For much of England's modern history, they've had some of the best midfielders in the world – players like Steven Gerrard, Frank Lampard, Paul Scholes and David Beckham. But those players couldn't always adapt to fit their talents into the same team.

When Bellingham broke into Birmingham City's first team, he added a new position to his game: the wing. "He played wide right, he played wide left," said teammate Paul Robinson. "For his development, he had the makings of playing in different positions higher up the pitch. Jude was always capable of doing that because of his brain."

Yes, Bellingham's game intelligence combined with his all-round technical skills meant he could adapt to any position or tactical system.

After starting on the wing, he moved into the number 8 position for Birmingham City's first team.

He started off there for Borussia Dortmund, too, but also filled in at number 4. By his second season, he had established himself as one of Borussia Dortmund's best attackers.

And for England, he's played as a number 4, 8, 10, and even on the left wing.

> ***"Jude gives us many tactical possibilities ... with him, different systems are possible."***
>
> LUCIEN FAVRE, BORUSSIA DORTMUND MANAGER

Bellingham's ability to play anywhere gives his managers options. Our number 22 discovered this when signing for Real Madrid, where he faced a whole new challenge...

ATHLETIC BILBAO 0 | 2 REAL MADRID

12 AUGUST 2023 • SAN MAMÉS, BILBAO

As Real Madrid lined up for their first game of the 2023–24 season, word spread around the stands. Manager Carlo Ancelotti had filled the gap left by legendary striker Karim Benzema's … with a midfielder!

How could a midfielder, new signing Jude Bellingham, play upfront?

As the game started, Bellingham patrolled high up the pitch. But he also tracked back to help in defence, playing as a number 10 and false 9 rolled into one. And in the 36th minute, his chance came. A David Alaba corner found its way to Bellingham, who instinctively volleyed towards the net. GOAL!

And Bellingham wasn't done there. His late runs into the penalty area created complete chaos. Real Madrid had found their new striker!

"He comes into the box like a motorbike," Ancelotti purred. And Bellingham was just as pleased with his performance.

"I have been really working on my timing getting into the box," added Jude. "And as I am arriving, I am arriving with big hunger." ■

WHO'S THE WINNER?

This one is surely too close to call. Let's call it an honourable tie for these two 10 out of 10s.

SO COME ON THEN... WHO IS THE SKILLS GOAT?

In this Skills section, we've looked at Kane and Bellingham's physical, technical and tactical skills. Now it's time to VOTE FOR THE GOAT. Up first: Seth to argue in favour of his fantastic finisher.

SETH'S CASE FOR KANE

To be a GOAT, you need to be the best in the world. Yes, Bellingham is very good at lots of things, but what is he *the best* at? Shooting? Ha, Kane's a world-leader when it comes to scoring.

He may not be the quickest, but you don't need to sprint if you're already in the right position. He may not dribble much, but what's the point of beating one player if you can beat an entire team with a clever pass or devastating strike?

This forward gives his all for the team, dropping selflessly into midfield to help teammates like Son score.

Sure, Bellingham runs about a lot too, but he's so desperate to use his wide-ranging skills that he can try too much without focusing on what actually wins games. And what actually wins games? The skills of my GOAT: Harry Kane.

MATT'S CASE FOR BELLINGHAM

Who would you rather have in your England football team: a striker with one skill, or a young maestro with many? If you're picking the first option, then sorry, I can't help you – welcome to 30 more years of hurt!

We all know what Kane is best at – scoring goals – but with Jude, we're still not quite sure because he's so great at EVERYTHING! Running, shooting, dribbling, tackling, passing, heading: there's nothing the kid can't do.

Strength, speed, skill, vision, determination, composure: this England GOAT has got it all!

Forget number 22; with his all-round talent and football brain, Bellingham is more of a 66 (that's the numbers 1 to 11 added together, by the way).

While Bellingham still has a long way to go to match Kane for consistency, he will, and he won't stop there. Bellingham is on his way to becoming not just England's best player now, but their GREATEST OF ALL TIME.

Matt
Shall I slow my argument down? It was probably too quick for Harry Kane.

Seth
Careful, Kane can finish anything. But he can save his legs on this one: you've finished yourself. What a rubbish argument!

Matt
I don't need to argue when everyone agrees with me about Bellingham.
I just speak common sense.

Seth
You missed "non" from that last word.

Matt
What does *sensenon* mean?

THE SCORES ARE IN:

	KANE	BELLINGHAM
PHYSICAL SKILLS	7/10	9/10
TECHNICAL SKILLS	10/10	9/10
TACTICAL SKILLS	10/10	10/10
TOTAL SCORE	27/30	28/30

So, those are our ratings, but now the power is in your hands. Who do you think is the GOAT when it comes to skills?

My Skills GOAT is

....

HALF-TIME

HALF-TIME

Eng-er-land, Eng-er-land, Eng-er-land! How lucky are we to have two fantastic players with such courageous character and silky skills wearing the Three Lions! And we haven't even talked about their scarily good stats or impressive contributions yet!

While we take a break to catch our breath, we're going to leave you with some half-time entertainment…

GENERAL KNOWLEDGE

1. Kane went to the same school and played for the same local boys' team as which former England captain?
2. How old was Bellingham when he made his debut for the Birmingham City first team – 16, 17 or 18?
3. What now-famous phrase did Bellingham shout after scoring a last-minute overhead kick against Slovakia at Euro 2024?
4. Kane broke the record for most Premier League goal combinations with which Tottenham Hotspur teammate?
5. When Kane missed a penalty against France at the 2022 World Cup, what did Bellingham do?

KANE OR BELLINGHAM? OR BOTH?

1. I made my England senior debut at the age of 17.

☐ Kane ☐ Bellingham ☐ Both

2. I scored on my England senior debut.

☐ Kane ☐ Bellingham ☐ Both

3. I've played for one of the biggest clubs in Germany.

☐ Kane ☐ Bellingham ☐ Both

4. I've played for a club in EFL League One.

☐ Kane ☐ Bellingham ☐ Both

5. My brother is also a professional footballer.

☐ Kane ☐ Bellingham ☐ Both

GENERAL KNOWLEDGE ANSWERS

1. David Beckham • 2. 16 • 3. "Who else?" • 4. Son Heung-Min
5. He put a supportive arm around his shoulder.

KANE OR BELLINGHAM? OR BOTH?

1. Bellingham • 2. Kane • 3. Both • 4. Kane • 5. Bellingham

KANE'S GREATEST GOALS

100 UP!

SOUTHAMPTON 0 | 2 TOTTENHAM HOTSPUR

19 DECEMBER 2015 • PREMIER LEAGUE

Kane celebrated his 100th game for Tottenham Hotspur in style as he slalomed past not one, not two, but three Southampton defenders, before placing the ball into the bottom corner of the net. ■

THE MASKED MAN STRIKES

TOTTENHAM HOTSPUR 2 | 2 ARSENAL

5 MARCH 2016 • PREMIER LEAGUE

Wearing a face mask to protect his broken nose, Kane hit a stunning, curling strike from an impossible angle to send Tottenham Hotspur top of the league (until North London rivals, Arsenal, equalized 14 minutes later)! ■

CHAMPIONS LEAGUE CLASS

TOTTENHAM HOTSPUR 3 | 1 BORUSSIA DORTMUND

13 SEPTEMBER 2017
CHAMPIONS LEAGUE

Kane was like a rampaging bull as he held off one defender on the halfway line, muscled his way past a second, then dribbled round a third before hitting a left-footed piledriver from just inside the area. ■

THE SHARPEST SCISSORS IN THE BOX

ENGLAND 5 | 0 ALBANIA

12 NOVEMBER 2021
EUROPEAN QUALIFIERS

Just before half-time, Kane lost his marker at a corner and unleashed a stunning scissor kick into the net. What a way to complete his fourth England hat-trick! ■

THE LONG-RANGE LEGEND

BAYERN MUNICH 8 | 0 DARMSTADT

28 OCTOBER 2023 • BUNDESLIGA

Another hat-trick, and the pick of the bunch was an incredible lob from inside Kane's own half! After controlling the ball with his left foot, Kane unleashed a wonderstrike with his right that was later voted Bundesliga Goal of the Season. ■

BELLINGHAM'S GREATEST GOALS

A SWEET JUDE SOLO

ARMINIA BIELEFELD 1 | 3 BORUSSIA DORTMUND

23 OCTOBER 2021 • BUNDESLIGA

Bellingham spun the first defender, glided past the second, then sat the third one down before chipping over keeper Stefan Ortega. It was a goal that saw comparisons to fellow GOAT candidate Lionel Messi. ■

SPIN TO WIN

BORUSSIA DORTMUND 6 | 0 WOLFSBURG

7 MAY 2023 • BUNDESLIGA

Bellingham charged into the Wolfsburg half before cutting inside and sending the defender for a hot dog! From 30 yards out, he let off a left-footed strike that rattled the bar, before bouncing and spinning into the net. ■

~~MARADONA~~ BELLINGHAM

NAPOLI 2 | 3 REAL MADRID

3 OCTOBER 2023 • CHAMPIONS LEAGUE

In the Diego Armando Maradona Stadium, Bellingham did his best impression of the Argentinian GOAT. Receiving the ball just inside the Napoli half, he glided past their entire defence (nutmegging the last man) before shooting into the far corner. ■

A CLÁSICO STRIKE

BARCELONA 1 | 2 REAL MADRID

28 OCTOBER 2023 • LA LIGA

Bellingham collected a clearance just outside the penalty area, shifted the ball onto his right foot, then let fly! Barcelona keeper Marc-André ter Stegen had no chance as Bellingham's curling shot nestled in the net. ■

HEAD-OVER-HEELS FOR JUDE

ENGLAND 2 | 1 SLOVAKIA

30 JUNE 2024
EUROPEAN CHAMPIONSHIPS ROUND OF 16

With England moments away from elimination, Bellingham threw himself at Marc Guéhi's flick on and scored a sensational bicycle kick goal that Kane later described as "the best in our [England's] history". ■

CHAMPIONS LEAGUE 2023-24 SEMI-FINAL:

THE CLÁSICO CLASH

Normally our GOATs are playing on the same team for England. But once they went head-to-head in the European Clásico, the name given to the historic rivalry between Kane's Bayern Munich and Bellingham's Real Madrid. The epic battle played out over two legs of a Champions League semi-final:

PENALTY PRESSURE

BAYERN MUNICH 5 | 3 REAL MADRID

FIRST LEG: 30 APRIL 2024
ALLIANZ ARENA, MUNICH

A tense game was tied at 1–1 when Bayern Munich were awarded a penalty in the 57th minute. Up stepped Kane, Bayern's trusted bagsman, for his big moment. "I know you're going to go to the keeper's left," Bellingham whispered as he attempted to put Kane off.

When the whistle blew, Kane ran forward, stuttered, and then struck the ball exactly where Bellingham was signalling. The keeper, Andriy Lunin, dived the other way. Goal! Kane charged to the corner in delight to celebrate with his teammates.

But a late Vinícius Júnior equalizer for Real Madrid meant it was all to play for in the second leg… ■

REAL RALLY FOR FIGHTBACK

REAL MADRID 2 | 1 BAYERN MUNICH

SECOND LEG: 8 MAY 2024
SANTIAGO BERNABÉU, MADRID

With 68 minutes gone and the game still tied, Kane picked out Alphonso Davies with a fantastic pass. Davies cut inside and shot to put Bayern Munich 1–0 up on the night, and 3–2 up on aggregate.

With just five minutes left, Bayern Munich manager Thomas Tuchel made a big decision. He substituted Harry Kane!

Just three minutes later, Bellingham received the ball in Bayern Munich's half, then played a pass to Vinícius Júnior. Manuel Neuer spilt his tame shot … straight to Real Madrid substitute Joselu, who tapped in. 1–1!

Now Real Madrid had the momentum, and in the 91st minute, the incredible comeback was complete as Joselu scored again to send Real Madrid through 4–3 on aggregate!

"When I was seven years old in Birmingham I was dreaming of nights like this," a jubilant Bellingham said, all smiles, at full time. ■

So that's the story of Kane and Bellingham greatest-ever clash. But soon we'll find out who wins their biggest battle yet: their GOAT battle! We've got two more chapters until we find out … so let's get cracking, starting with Stats.

STATS

WHAT ARE FOOTBALL STATS?

Stats (full name: statistics) are facts expressed through numbers, and these days, they're everywhere in the world of football.

Stats can tell us a lot about a player. How? Well, loads of footballers have fantastic skills, but only the true GOATs know how to make the most of their super powers, game after game, year after year.

Kane and Bellingham have both recorded big numbers on the pitch, but which are the ones that matter most? We're going to break their key stats down into three main categories:

PERFORMANCE STATS
We'll focus on the two biggest numbers: goals and assists.

INDIVIDUAL ACHIEVEMENTS
We'll add up their achievements – everything from Golden Boots to Player of the Year awards.

TEAM STATS
We'll analyse the cups and league titles won, for clubs and country.

Are you ready to find out which England superstar will be crowned GOAT of the big game stats?

PERFORMANCE STATS

KANE

	GAMES	GOALS	ASSISTS
FOR CLUB	603	386	101
FOR COUNTRY	105	71	19
TOTAL	708	457	120

BELLINGHAM

	GAMES	GOALS	ASSISTS
FOR CLUB	268	64	52
FOR COUNTRY	42	6	10
TOTAL	310	70	62

It shouldn't come as a big shock to hear that Kane is the GOAT with the most overall goal contributions (goals and assists) because:

- He's a striker, whereas Bellingham is more of a midfielder.
- He's nearly ten years older, so he's played way more games.

OK, so what if we make this battle a little fairer by comparing their goal contribution stats per game instead? *Hmmm*, sorry, Bellingham, Kane is still the clear winner here:

GOAL CONTRIBUTIONS PER GAME

	KANE	BELLINGHAM
GOALS PER GAME	0.65	0.23
ASSISTS PER GAME	0.17	0.20
GOAL CONTRIBUTIONS PER GAME	0.82	0.43

So case closed: Kane is the England stats king? No, no, it's time to dig down deeper…

HARRY KANE

Two things that really stand out about Kane's club stats are firstly just what a consistent goalscorer he's been and secondly how he's added more assists to his game over the years:

SEASON	CLUB	GOALS	ASSISTS
2014–15	Tottenham Hotspur	31	6
2015–16	Tottenham Hotspur	28	2
2016–17	Tottenham Hotspur	35	7
2017–18	Tottenham Hotspur	41	5
2018–19	Tottenham Hotspur	24	6

2019–20	Tottenham Hotspur	24	2
2020–21	Tottenham Hotspur	33	17
2021–22	Tottenham Hotspur	27	10
2022–23	Tottenham Hotspur	32	6
2023–24	Bayern Munich	44	12
2024–25	Bayern Munich	37	12

Even during the "worst" of his 11 seasons at the highest level, Harry still scored 24 goals! His lowest-ever tally in a Premier League season? 17 goals, which actually matches Manchester United forward Marcus Rashford's best-ever season!

In total, Harry Kane scored 213 Premier League goals, putting him second behind Alan Shearer in the all-time top-scorer list. And in terms of goals *per game*, he takes first place:

PREMIER LEAGUE GOALS PER GAME

PLAYER	GOALS	GAMES	GOALS PER GAME
ALAN SHEARER	260	441	0.59
HARRY KANE	213	320	0.67
WAYNE ROONEY	208	491	0.42
ANDREW COLE	187	415	0.45
MO SALAH	185	297	0.62

JUDE BELLINGHAM

While Bellingham will never be a sharp-shooting striker quite like Kane, it's also important to remember that he has played in different roles for different teams – from defensive midfield through to centre forward – and his position on the pitch makes a massive difference to his performance stats.

For Birmingham City, Bellingham mostly played as a central (rather than attacking) midfielder, and that's reflected in the stats:

BIRMINGHAM CITY

SEASON	GAMES	GOALS	ASSISTS
2019–20	44	4	2

After his first season at Borussia Dortmund, Jadon Sancho was sold, so Bellingham stepped forwards and got more creative in midfield. Then by Bellingham's third season, Erling Haaland had gone too, so Bellingham pushed even further up the pitch and took over as his team's top scorer:

BORUSSIA DORTMUND

SEASON	GAMES	GOALS	ASSISTS
2020–21	46	4	4
2021–22	44	6	14
2022–23	42	14	7

In his debut season at Real Madrid, Bellingham took his attacking game to the next level. He often played as a false 9/centre forward, and just look at the stats!

REAL MADRID

SEASON	GAMES	GOALS	ASSISTS
2023–24	43	23	13

But even when he plays further forwards, there's a whole lot more to Bellingham's high-energy game than just goals and assists. During the 2023–24 La Liga season, he also averaged per game:

- 1.94 dribbles (the third most at Real Madrid behind the Brazilians Vinícius Júnior and Rodrygo)
- 1.86 key passes (behind only top playmakers Toni Kroos and Luka Modrić)
- 1.7 tackles (more than star defender Antonio Rüdiger!)
- 0.77 interceptions

When Kylian Mbappé arrived at Real Madrid in summer 2024 to take over the number 9 striker position, Bellingham dropped back into an attacking midfield role again, leading to fewer goals but more assists.

REAL MADRID

SEASON	GAMES	GOALS	ASSISTS
2024–25	52	14	14

Two England GOATs – one a great goalscorer, the other an amazing all-rounder – but whose performance stats are better when the pressure is really on? It's time for a … BIG-GAME HEAD-TO-HEAD, starting with their clubs!

BIG CLUB GAMES

KANE

	GAMES	GOALS	ASSISTS	GOAL CONTRIBUTION PER GAME
CUP FINALS	4	0	0	0.00
CHAMPIONS LEAGUE KNOCK-OUT GAMES	19	11	3	0.74
TOTTENHAM HOTSPUR V. ARSENAL (NORTH LONDON DERBY)	19	14	2	0.84
BAYERN MUNICH V. BORUSSIA DORTMUND (DER KLASSIKER)	4	3	0	0.75
TOTAL	46	28	5	**0.72**

BELLINGHAM

	GAMES	GOALS	ASSISTS	GOAL CONTRIBUTION PER GAME
CUP FINALS	7	0	4	0.57
CHAMPIONS LEAGUE KNOCK-OUT GAMES	17	2	2	0.24
BORUSSIA DORTMUND V. BAYERN MUNICH (DER KLASSIKER)	8	0	4	0.50
REAL MADRID V. BARCELONA (EL CLÁSICO)	7	3	1	0.57
TOTAL	39	5	11	**0.41**

This means that on average, Kane contributes 0.72 goals per game and Bellingham contributes 0.41 goals per game. So while Kane still comes out on top in terms of goal contributions per game, the gap between the two GOATs is now shrinking.

In the matches that matter most, Bellingham's stats stay almost the same, but Kane's drop – mainly due to his four cup-final failures.

So, what happens when we compare their big-game performance stats for England?

BIG COUNTRY GAMES

KANE

	GAMES	GOALS	ASSISTS	GOAL CONTRIBUTION PER GAME
ALL MATCHES AT MAJOR TOURNAMENTS	29	15	3	0.62
KNOCK-OUT MATCHES	14	9	0	0.64
TOURNAMENT FINALS	2	0	0	0.00

BELLINGHAM

	GAMES	GOALS	ASSISTS	GOAL CONTRIBUTION PER GAME
ALL MATCHES AT MAJOR TOURNAMENTS	15	3	2	0.33
KNOCK-OUT MATCHES	7	1	2	0.43
TOURNAMENT FINALS	1	0	1	1.00

Oooh, interesting! And if you take out Bellingham's numbers from Euro 2020, where he was only used as a late sub, his England stats get even closer to Kane's:

	GAMES	GOALS	ASSISTS	GOAL CONTRIBUTION PER GAME
ALL MATCHES AT MAJOR TOURNAMENTS	12	3	2	0.42
KNOCK-OUT MATCHES	6	1	2	0.50
TOURNAMENT FINALS	1	0	1	1.00

Yes, when it comes to grabbing big goals and assists in the biggest games for his country, Bellingham has already shown that he's the midfield man for the job. And with the major international tournaments getting bigger and bigger, surely his stats are only going to get better and better…

ENGLAND INSIGHT: WORLD CUP TEAMS

Until 1982, the World Cup was limited to 16 teams, which made it more difficult to qualify (England failed to do so in 1974 and 1978), and meant a maximum of six matches. By the 2022 World Cup, however, the number of teams had risen to 32, and so Kane and Bellingham had already played five matches each when England exited in the quarter-finals. At the 2026 World Cup, there will be 48 countries competing for the trophy, which means even more games and even more chances for our superstars to score goals!

WHO'S THE WINNER?

Despite Bellingham's age and big-game mentality, he still can't beat Kane when it comes to football's killer performance stats. The guy's a goalscoring machine!

These numbers are only one way to decide which football GOAT is the greatest, though; let's move on and look at some more…

INDIVIDUAL ACHIEVEMENTS

Let's look at how many individual awards each of our England GOATs has won so far:

	AWARDS	KANE	BELLINGHAM
INDIVIDUAL	*Golden Boy Award (best youngster of the year who's playing in Europe)*	*0*	*1*
	Kopa Trophy (basically the junior Ballon d'Or!)	*0*	*1*
	Gerd Müller Trophy (for best striker of the year)	*1*	*0*
CLUB	*League Best Player of the Year*	*1*	*2*
	League Best Young Player of the Year	*1*	*2*
	League Golden Boot (most goals)	*5*	*0*
	League Top Playmaker (most assists)	*1*	*0*
	Champions League Young Player of the Season	*0*	*1*
	Champions League Top Scorer	*1*	*0*
	Champions League Team of the Season	*1*	*1*
	European Golden Shoe (for top scorer in Europe's top leagues)	*1*	*0*
COUNTRY	*World Cup Golden Boot*	*1*	*0*
	Euros Golden Boot	*1*	*0*
	England Player of the Year	*2*	*0*
	TOTAL	*16*	*8*

Let's start with the headline news:

- The GOAT with the most Player of the Year awards is **BELLINGHAM!**
- The GOAT with the most Golden Boot awards is **KANE!**

And while neither player has won the Ballon d'Or – the annual award for world's best footballer – (yet, anyway), the GOAT with the highest finish in the voting for the award so far is … **BELLINGHAM!**

BALLON D'OR RANKING

KANE	BELLINGHAM
10th, in 2017, 2018 and 2024	3rd, in 2024

But before we make a decision, it's time to take a closer look at the stories behind some of our GOATs' biggest individual achievements…

KANE'S GOLDEN BOOTS

During his nine seasons at Tottenham Hotspur, Kane won the Premier League Golden Boot award – given to the player who scores the most goals during the season – an impressive three times (and finished runner-up twice).

KICK-OFF
CHARACTER
SKILLS
HALF-TIME
STATS
CONTRIBUTION
EXTRA TIME

To put that into context, only Thierry Henry and Mo Salah have won the Premier League Golden Boot more times (four) than Kane.

At Bayern Munich, Kane has taken his sharp shooting to an even higher level. In his first season in Germany, he finished as top scorer in both the Bundesliga (36 goals) AND the Champions League (8 goals)!

In international football, Kane has won two England Player of the Year awards (back-to-back in 2017 and 2018), plus two World Cup Golden Boots.

ENGLAND INSIGHT: GOLDEN BOOTS

Since the country's first major tournament, the 1950 World Cup, only three England players have ever come home with a Golden Boot: Gary Lineker at the 1986 World Cup, Alan Shearer at Euro 1996, and Harry Kane – twice – at the 2018 World Cup and then Euro 2024.

But arguably Kane's proudest moment for his country actually came between those two major tournaments…

KANE, ENGLAND'S GOALSCORING GOAT

ITALY 1 | 2 ENGLAND

23 MARCH 2023
STADIO DIEGO ARMANDO MARADONA, NAPLES

England were already winning 1–0 in this tricky Euro 2024 qualifier when, just before half-time, Kane chested the ball down in the box and it bounced off a defender's arm. Handball! Penalty!

Of course, it was Captain Kane himself who stepped up to the spot and … he calmly sent Italy's giant keeper Gianluigi Donnarumma the wrong way. GOAL! 2–0 to England!

And it wasn't just any old international goal for Kane: it was his record-breaking 54th (and in only 81 games) to take him past Wayne Rooney, as England's new all-time top male goalscorer! So once the ball was safely nestled in the net, Kane raced over to the corner flag, kissing the Three Lions on his shirt and roaring with delight.

Three days later at Wembley, Kane was presented with a special trophy to mark his amazing achievement, and guess what it was… Yes, another Golden Boot! ■

BELLINGHAM'S PLAYER OF THE YEAR AWARDS

"Being involved in every aspect of the game is better than being greedy for goals," Bellingham once said, and that all-action attitude is why Bellingham is always a leading candidate when it comes to Player of the Year awards. In fact, his success rate so far is simply ridiculous:

2019–20

Following his one and only season for the Birmingham City first team, he was named the club's Young Player of the Year and the Young Player of the Season for the whole EFL (the Championship, plus Leagues One and Two)!

2020–21

In his debut season at Borussia Dortmund, Bellingham picked up the Bundesliga Newcomer of the Season prize.

2021–22

In his second season in Germany, Bellingham was selected in the Bundesliga Team of the Season, and there was something even better to come…

BELLINGHAM, THE BEST IN THE BUNDESLIGA ... AND BEYOND!

BORUSSIA DORTMUND 4 | 3 AUGSBURG

22 JANUARY 2023
WESTFALENSTADION, DORTMUND

After back-to-back defeats, Borussia Dortmund had slipped down to sixth in the Bundesliga table. With Sancho and Haaland both gone, who could step up to fill that superstar gap?

Bursting forward from midfield in the 30th minute, Bellingham was determined to be that man. With a drop of the shoulder, he shifted the ball to the right and then blasted a shot from the edge of the box into the bottom corner. 1–0 to Borussia Dortmund! 49 crazy minutes later, it was 3–3, until up leapt Bellingham to set up the winner.

One goal, one assist and 22 duels won – what a midfield masterclass, and what an important player Bellingham was becoming at Borussia Dortmund. Over the next few months, he helped push his team past Bayern Munich to the top of the table. But with just two games to go, Bellingham injured his knee, and without their main man, Borussia Dortmund fell apart, handing the title to Bayern Munich. Bellingham was left in tears.

All was not lost, though. Bellingham's eight goals, four assists, 98 tackles, 482 duels won and average of 2.8 successful dribbles per game (the joint-most with Bayer Leverkusen's Florian Wirtz) earned him the Bundesliga Player of the Season award. ■

Bellingham also finished second for the England Senior Men's Player of the Year award in 2023 and 2024.

Then guess what happened when he moved to Real Madrid in 2023... Yep, he won the La Liga Player of the Season award straight away!

WHO'S THE WINNER?

While Kane is the undisputed GOAT of the Golden Boot, we're giving the overall top spot to Bellingham for winning so many individual awards at such a young age.

But as Bellingham said himself in 2023, "For me, the important thing is team trophies."

So, let's take a look at those now, shall we?

TEAM STATS

		KANE	BELLINGHAM
CLUB	CHAMPIONS LEAGUE	0	1
	LEAGUE TITLES	1	1
	DOMESTIC CUPS	0	2
	UEFA SUPER CUP	0	1
	FIFA INTERCONTINENTAL CUP	0	1
COUNTRY	FIFA WORLD CUP	0	0
	UEFA EUROS	0	0
TOTAL		1	6

So first, a look at the main headlines:

- The GOAT who has won the most team trophies is **BELLINGHAM!**
- But when it comes to league titles … **IT'S A TIE!**
- The only GOAT to win the Champions League (so far) is **BELLINGHAM!**

Interesting! Let's take a closer look at who is our team trophies GOAT.

HARRY KANE

WHAT THE DOUBTERS SAY

"Kane's not a GOAT because his teams never win anything!"

WRONG!

"Here is a man who has performed to a relentlessly high level while playing for Spurs and England, two teams with almost no modern history of winning pots."

BARNEY RONAY, FOOTBALL WRITER

Kane has fired his clubs and country to SIX finals, but sadly due to injuries, excellent opponents, penalty shoot-outs, and dodgy decisions, poor Harry has NEVER finished on the winning side, or even scored a goal.

UNLUCKY KANE

- 2015 League Cup final against Chelsea: he had a shot brilliantly blocked by John Terry.
- 2019 Champions League final against Liverpool: Tottenham Hotspur conceded a controversial penalty after just 24 seconds.

- 2021 League Cup final against Manchester City: a half-fit Kane couldn't save Tottenham Hotspur from a late defeat.
- Euro 2020 final against Italy: he scored England's first penalty but they lost the shoot-out.
- 2023 German Super Cup against RB Leipzig (Kane's Bayern Munich debut): when he came on as a second-half substitute, his team were already 2–0 down.
- Euro 2024 against Spain: struggling with a lower back injury, Kane were subbed off after 60 minutes.

Harry also finished second in the Premier League with Tottenham Hotspur in 2016–17, and then third in the Bundesliga with Bayern Munich in 2023–24.

But just when it looked like "The Kane Curse" might be real, his long wait came to an end...

For the 2024–25 season, Bayern Munich brought in a new manager, Vincent Kompany, and several new signings. But up front, they had the same superstar striker, with the same burning ambition: to finally win his first major trophy. Kane and his teammates would have three chances in three different competitions – so, how many could they take?

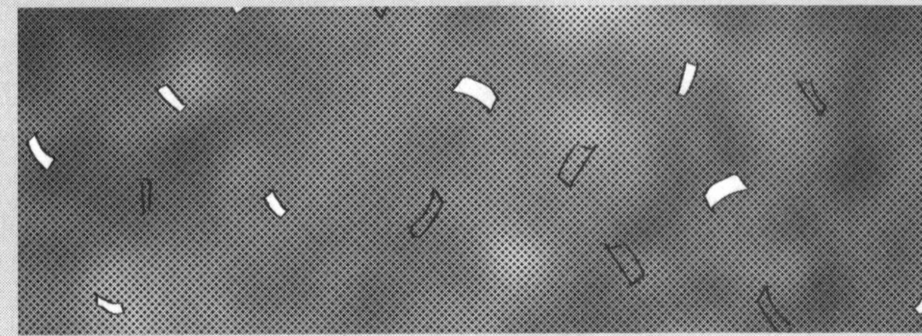

In December, Bayern Munich lost to Bayer Leverkusen in the German Cup round of 16, and then in April, they were beaten by Inter Milan in the Champions League quarter-finals. Oh dear, that left only one last trophy: the Bundesliga title. Could Bayern Munich keep calm and lift it for the 34th time?

While their rivals Bayer Leverkusen were struggling to convert draws into victories, Steady Harry helped his team to get the games won. After 14 goals and seven assists in his first 11 league matches (including three hat-tricks!), Kane's scoring had slowed down a little, but not much. He ended up scoring:

- *The winner against Borussia Mönchengladbach*
- *Two headers against Holstein Kiel*
- *Two penalties against Werder Bremen*

The most important thing, however, was the team. At the back, Bayern Munich looked more solid than last season, and in attack, they had plenty of other world-class matchwinners, like Leroy Sané, Michael Olise, Jamal Musiala and Thomas Müller.

So when Kane found himself suspended (he had five yellow cards across the season) with Bayern Munich just three points

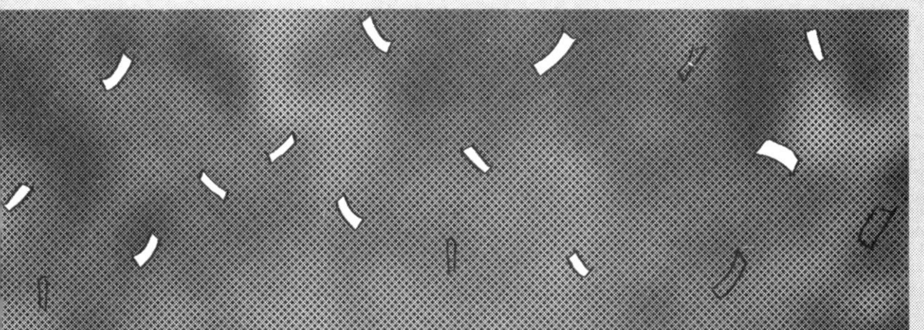

away from the Bundesliga title, he was sad but not too worried. Though Bayern Munich had lost three of the six games they'd played without Kane in the starting line-up, he still trusted his teammates to get the game (and the league) won without him.

At half-time against RB Leipzig, Bayern were losing 2–0, but they fought back to lead 3–2 with seconds to go. Surely this was it? Kane was on the touchline in his tracksuit, ready to rush onto the pitch and celebrate his first trophy with his teammates, but no, in the last minute, Leipzig equalized.

In the end, Kane only had one extra day to wait. Another Leverkusen draw handed the Bundesliga title to Bayern Munich, and at last, after 12 years of trying, Harry had finally won his first major team trophy. What a magical moment!

For his epic contribution to his team's success, Kane was named as the Bundesliga's Player of the Season (as well as the league's top scorer for the second consecutive season). But for Kane it was all about his team.

A man of few words, Kane chose to express his delight through an emoji – a gold trophy – and a video of him and his teammates celebrating together. The song they were singing? "We Are the Champions" of course! ■

BELLINGHAM

WHAT THE DOUBTERS SAY

"Sure, Bellingham has won a few top trophies, but that's only because he plays for Real Madrid, the best team in the world!"

It's true that Bellingham has already played with some of the greatest footballers ever. Look at the line-up of Bellingham's dream teammates, chosen from his club and international career.

> ***"When you have great players on your side, your game becomes better. Jude spent his first season at Madrid with Modrić and Toni Kroos."***
>
> PAUL LAMBERT, FORMER BORUSSIA DORTMUND PLAYER

But Bellingham didn't just fluke his way into the Real Madrid midfield. He earned his place with his stand-out performances at each stage of his football journey: first at Birmingham City and then at Borussia Dortmund.

BELLINGHAM'S DREAM TEAMMATES

Thibaut Courtois
(Real Madrid)

Kyle Walker
(England)

Antonio Rüdiger
(Real Madrid)

Manuel Akanji
(Borussia Dortmund)

David Alaba
(Real Madrid)

Luka Modrić
(Real Madrid)

Declan Rice
(England)

Toni Kroos
(Real Madrid)

Kylian Mbappé
(Real Madrid)

Erling Haaland
(Borussia Dortmund)

Vinícius Júnior
(Real Madrid)

Subs: Jordan Pickford (England), Dani Carvajal (Real Madrid), Mats Hummels (Borussia Dortmund), Fede Valverde (Real Madrid), Phil Foden (England), Bukayo Saka (England), Harry Kane (England)

At Real Madrid, he got off to a stunning start, scoring ten goals in his first ten league games! But how did his debut season end? Let's see the huge impact he had on the best team in the world...

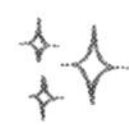

TREBLE JOY FOR JUDE

From his first day at Real Madrid, Bellingham had made his ambition very clear: to win trophies. During the 2023–24 season, the club would be competing in four different competitions: the Spanish Super Cup, the Copa del Rey, La Liga and the Champions League. How many of these trophies could Bellingham collect?

Number one arrived in January 2024, as Real Madrid thrashed their big rivals, Barcelona, 4–1 to lift the Spanish Super Cup. While Vinícius Júnior was the hat-trick hero, Bellingham set up his opening goal with a defence-splitting pass.

Four days later, Real were knocked out of the Copa del Rey by their Madrid rivals, Atlético. But the treble was still on, and Bellingham and his teammates were determined to achieve it.

Next up: a 36th La Liga title. Bellingham set up a late winner for Dani Carvajal against UD Almería, scored two goals of his own against Girona, and then, with his team drawing 2–2 with Barcelona at the Bernabéu, Bellingham burst into the box and blasted home another last-minute winner!

It was Bellingham's 21st goal of the season (in all competitions), taking him above David Beckham as Real Madrid's new all-time leading English scorer. Soon the La Liga title was in the bag and he was celebrating his second trophy for the club. Yes, Los Blancos were *Campeones de España*!

And Bellingham's sensational first season wasn't over yet. There was still one more trophy to win, the biggest of them all: the Champions League…

After scoring four in his first four European games for Real Madrid, the goals had dried up for Bellingham. Instead, he created chances for the team's other amazing attackers:

- Vinícius Júnior in the round of 16 against RB Leipzig
- Rodrygo in the quarter-finals against Manchester City
- Joselu in the semi-finals against Kane's Bayern Munich

Real Madrid were through to another Champions League final against his old club, Borussia Dortmund. Bellingham did what big-game players do: make a difference for their team. In the 83rd minute, he set up Vinícius Júnior to score the crucial second goal. Before the ball even hit the net, Jude was already throwing his arms high into the sky. Real Madrid were the Champions of Europe yet again, and their treble was complete!

"It's got to be up there in terms of the perfect season," a smiling Jude said afterwards. "It's the best night of my life." ■

WHO'S THE WINNER?

While Kane is much better than his medal count suggests, this section is all about team trophies, so we've got to give it to Bellingham, haven't we? The guy won a treble at the age of 20, and playing for Real Madrid, there'll surely be plenty more to come.

SO COME ON THEN... WHO IS THE STATS GOAT?

In this Stats section, we've looked at Kane and Bellingham's records for goals and assists, and what each player has achieved as an individual and a team member. Now it's time to put all that knowledge into action and VOTE FOR THE GOAT!

Now over to Seth to make the case for Mr Consistent Kane...

SETH'S CASE FOR KANE

So in terms of stats, Bellingham has had ONE good season where his incredible teammates won him the Champions League and a couple of domestic trophies. And just how many goal contributions did he manage in that best-ever season?! It was 25.

In Kane's *worst*-ever season since becoming a first-team regular, he made 26 goal contributions. What's best-ever for one supposed GOAT would rank as worst-ever for the true stats GOAT.

I like my GOATs to be consistently brilliant, and there's nobody out there who's more consistent than Kane. Game after game, season after season, this GOAT delivers. He's Tottenham Hotspur's all-time top scorer, England's all-time top men's scorer, and still he keeps on scoring!

His performance stats are through the roof. He's won more individual awards than Bellingham. And though he paid a big price for his loyalty to Tottenham Hotspur when it comes to team trophies, he's simply let Bellingham have a head-start. Watch out, Jude, Harry's coming to overtake you on trophies won, too!

MATT'S CASE FOR BELLINGHAM

Kane v. Bellingham in a battle of the big football stats? Too easy! The winner is clear, and here's a clue: he's not the England captain … yet!

Bellingham's numbers really do speak for themselves, but let me repeat them one more time, just in case, like Seth, you haven't been listening.

In just six seasons as a professional footballer, Jude has already:

- Scored over 70 goals for clubs and country, despite playing in a variety of different positions.
- Won nine individual awards, including the Player of the Season awards in both Germany and Spain.
- Lifted six team trophies, including the La Liga title AND the Champions League.

Sorry, Seth, but Kane could play until he's 80, and he still wouldn't win that one!

So, there you have it: Bellingham's stats already blow Kane out of Wembley Stadium, and the great news for England fans is that this GOAT is only just getting started.

Seth
Hey, if Harry had moved to Real Madrid or Manchester City, he would have won just as many trophies as Bellingham, if not more!

Matt
Yeah, and if I was better at making money, I'd be a millionaire.

Seth
Ha, don't be silly!

Matt
I know you are, but what am I?

Seth
A pain in the bum.

THE SCORES ARE IN:

	KANE	BELLINGHAM
PERFORMANCE STATS RATING	9/10	8/10
INDIVIDUAL ACHIEVEMENTS RATING	8/10	9/10
TEAM STATS RATING	7/10	9/10
TOTAL SCORE	24/30	26/30

So, those are our opinions, whether you wanted to hear them or not. Now it's your turn to have your say! When it comes to the stats, who do you think is the football GOAT – Kane or Bellingham?

My Stats GOAT is

....

CONTRIBUTION

WHAT IS CONTRIBUTION?

Here's another stat for you: you're now 75 per cent of your way through this football battle! You've already read about our GOATs' characters, skills and stats. Now it's time to analyse how much of a difference Kane and Bellingham have made.

To answer that massive question, we're going to break their contributions into three key categories:

CLUB LEVEL
We'll look at the impact Kane and Bellingham have had on the various teams they've played for.

COUNTRY
We'll review the impact they've had on England.

THE GAME
And finally, we'll assess how they've changed football itself.

So before we blow full-time on this book, let's decide our Contribution GOAT…

CLUB LEVEL

While one of our GOATs stayed at the same club for ten seasons (or 19 if you include his academy and loan years), the other has represented three clubs in just four years. They may now both be playing for top European teams, but their journeys couldn't have been more different. So what have they contributed to their clubs along the way?

HARRY KANE

For good reason, Tottenham Hotspur became known as the "Harry Kane Team".

> ***"We saw again, the Harry Kane team scores every day two or three goals."***
>
> PEP GUARDIOLA,
> MANCHESTER CITY MANAGER, 2017

While we can confirm that Tottenham Hotspur did indeed have another ten players on their team, there's no denying Kane's humungous contribution to his club.

He led Spurs to second place in the 2016–17 Premier League season, their best finish in 50 years.

In the nine seasons Kane was a regular starter, Spurs finished in the top four on five occasions. In their 22 Premier League seasons before Kane's debut, Spurs had finished in the top four just twice.

Before Kane, Spurs had made the knockout stages of the Champions League just twice: in 1961–62 and 2010–11. With Kane, they managed it four times, most notably in 2018–19, when they reached the final for the first time in their history!

Spurs won 54.9 per cent of the games Kane played in. For the games he was unavailable, their win rate dropped to 44.4 per cent.

He even scored a few goals – and broke a few records – along the way…

267 OF THE BEST FOR KANE

As Harry entered his final season for Tottenham Hotspur, the 2022–23 season, there was one club record left that he hadn't broken. It was for Spurs' all-time top goalscorer.

Nobody in the club's history had scored more than Jimmy Greaves' 266 goals, a record set *waaay* back in 1970.

But just over 50 years later, Kane had a chance of breaking it. He would start the 2022–23 season with 250 Spurs goals. Could this be the year he wrote his name into the club's history books?

Four goals in his first four games suggested he could – and the goals kept on coming! It was 12 by Christmas, 15 by the first week of January. Suddenly, Kane was just one goal away from Greaves' record!

Could he break the record in his next match: at home to Arsenal in the North London derby? No! Arsenal won 2–0 to leave Kane doubly frustrated.

Spurs would have to bounce back in their next match, away to Fulham. And thanks to Harry, they did! Kane's goal equalled Greaves' record and gave Spurs a 1–0 win.

Up next were Premier League champions, Manchester City, and Kane had one thing on his mind: winning. Oh, and he wouldn't mind breaking that record, too…

"THIS WAS HARRY KANE MAKING THE ART OF GOAL-SCORING LOOK LIKE THE EASIEST THING IN THE WORLD."

JACOB STEINBERG, *GUARDIAN*

After just 15 minutes, his chance came. Pierre-Emile Højbjerg found Kane inside the box. Instinctively, Kane struck a first-time right-footed shot … which bounced past Manchester City's keeper Ederson … and into the net. Goal!

The crowd went wild as Kane jumped for joy. And to make the day EVEN better, his historic goal was enough to secure Spurs a 1–0 victory. Hooray for Harry! ■

♪♪

"HE'S OUR ONE-SEASON WONDER, HE'S THE BEST WE'VE EVER KNOWN, HE'S ENGLAND'S TOP GOALSCORER, AND HE'S ONE OF OUR OWN!"

SPURS FANS' SONG FOR HARRY KANE

♪♪

JUDE BELLINGHAM

We know Bellingham's incredible impact at Real Madrid, winning La Liga, the Spanish Super Cup and the Champions League, but what about his two clubs before that?

BIRMINGHAM CITY'S NUMBER 22 FOR EVER

On 23 July 2020, Birmingham City made a surprise announcement: "In such a remarkably short space of time Jude has become an iconic figure at the Blues, showing what can be achieved through talent, hard work and dedication … the club have decided it would be fitting to retire Jude's number, to remember one of our own and to inspire others."

What? He was going to be only the third player since World Cup winner Bobby Moore to have their shirt retired by an English football club. Had he *really* contributed that much to his hometown club?!

Well, in many ways he had…

In his ten years at the Birmingham City academy, Bellingham could have signed for any bigger club that he liked. But instead he stayed loyal, not moving until he had signed a professional contract with Birmingham so the cash-strapped club could receive a transfer fee for him.

Although he didn't win any trophies or promotions during his one season in the first team, Jude crammed a LOT into a short period. At 16 years and 38 days, he became Birmingham City's youngest player of all time, and after playing in 44 games (scoring four goals and assisting twice), he helped them avoid relegation and was named as the EFL Young Player of the Season.

> ***"He was a very important player on the pitch, but also as a symbol of the club."***
>
> PEP CLOTET, BIRMINGHAM CITY MANAGER

Now, the inspiring story of the hometown hero would live on through his retired 22 shirt.

MAKING A DIFFERENCE AT DORTMUND

Borussia Dortmund made Bellingham the most expensive 17-year-old in history when they signed him in 2020 for £25 million. Worth it? You bet!

In his debut season he started in 33 of Borussia Dortmund's 51 games, including their German Cup final win against RB Leipzig – their first trophy in four years! As a result, he was voted by his fellow players as the Bundesliga's Newcomer of the Year.

The following season, Bellingham made the Bundesliga's team of the season, and in his third season he became Borussia Dortmund's youngest-ever captain, the team's top scorer, AND won the Bundesliga's Player of the Season award. Plus, if he hadn't been injured for the crunch final game against Mainz, Borussia Dortmund would probably have won their first Bundesliga title in 11 years!

"The fans of Dortmund want to see emotional, aggressive football and Jude fitted in perfectly."

OLIVER MÜLLER, GERMAN FOOTBALL WRITER

After playing his last game for the club, he was still able to make one mega final contribution to Borussia Dortmund: a massive transfer fee, reportedly of over €113 million!

COUNTRY

Kane and Bellingham may not have won a major international trophy yet, but what have they contributed to their national team so far?

ENGLAND INSIGHT: A HISTORY OF HURT

England's men's football team has had lots of world-class players, but not many world-class wins. The biggest underachievers played in the 2000s. With players such as Wayne Rooney, Steven Gerrard, Frank Lampard, Rio Ferdinand, and David Beckham, the team were considered so good it was called the "Golden Generation". However, they got knocked out in the quarter-finals at the 2002 and 2006 World Cups and Euro 2004 ... then didn't even qualify for Euro 2008!

A NEW LOW FOR ENGLAND

Despite a promising start to Kane's England career with a goal on his international debut, he soon suffered the same fate as the Golden Generation. After making his international debut in a 4–0 win over Lithuania in 2015, he arrived at Euro 2016 as England's main man and the favourite to finish as the tournament's top scorer. Could this be his tournament?

No! A tired Kane played just 240 of a possible 360 minutes and didn't even score. At times he had to fill in on the right wing and was even asked to take corners. England limped through the group stage, earning a knockout match against Iceland, a nation of just 330,000 people … and lost 2–1!

> ***"We are not a nation with a culture of winning at the European Championship and the World Cup."***
>
> STEVEN GERRARD, FORMER ENGLAND CAPTAIN

BBC pundit and former player Alan Shearer called it "the worst performance I've ever seen from an England team." Could England ever recover?

DID YOU KNOW? Between 2008 and 2016, England won just four matches out of 15 at major tournaments. None of those victories were in the knockout rounds.

CAPTAIN KANE

Given the captain's armband under new manager Gareth Southgate in 2017, Kane led England into a new era of success, pulling them back from their Icelandic low.

On the pitch Kane scored and created. There was his crucial late equalizer in a 2–2 draw against Scotland in his first game as captain. Then two goals and an assist in a 4–0 victory over Malta and the winning goals against Slovenia and Lithuania in important World Cup qualifying matches.

"We can all see the difference he has made for England."

MARTA, BRAZIL LEGEND

Off the pitch, Kane worked with Southgate to make the changing room a happy, welcoming place. "I've always wanted the environment to feel chilled out, in the sense that the guys can be themselves," he said.

With seven wins, four draws and just one defeat in the 12 games since Kane became captain, England were back on form. But could they do it on the biggest stage? Yes! At the 2018 World Cup, England made the semi-finals for the first time since 1990 (and just the third time in history), with Kane winning the Golden Boot for his six goals.

And this was no one-tournament wonder. At Euro 2020, Kane scored four goals in four knockout games as England reached their first final since 1966 … only to lose on penalties (although Kane scored his).

And this England team were about to get even better…

KANE AND BELLINGHAM

Jude Bellingham was just 17 years old at the start of Euro 2020 and had to make do with a place on England's bench.

But by the 2022 World Cup, he'd established himself in England's starting line-up. With Kane leading the line and Bellingham dominating midfield, their 12 goals in their first four games showed just how talented England's new-look team were. But a quarter final against France proved too much and England lost 2–1.

Would they get more at Euro 2024? After scoring just two goals in three group stage games, England found themselves 1–0 down to Slovakia in their round of 16 tie. As the clock ticked on, it was time for one of these GOATs to write themselves into the England history books…

ENGLAND 2 | 1 SLOVAKIA

30 JUNE 2024 • VELTINS-ARENA, GERMANY

By the 95th minute, England's players were desperate. They were 1–0 down and facing another embarrassing Euros exit that would rival their defeat to Iceland in 2016. So when they won a throw-in near Slovakia's goal, they packed the box with players.

Kyle Walker launched the throw into the box … Marc Guéhi flicked the ball on with his head … and then Bellingham, with his back to goal, powered himself into the air and unleashed an unstoppable bicycle kick into the net.

GOAL! And what a goal. Bellingham had not just saved England. He'd scored one of the most stunning and memorable

goals England fans had ever seen.

"Who else?!" he yelled in celebration, before standing with his arms held wide next to his captain, Harry Kane, who copied Bellingham's signature pose.

Minutes later, the comeback was complete in extra time when Kane headed in England's winner. Once again, Kane and Bellingham celebrated together. They were through to the next round!

After triumphing over Slovakia, England made it all the way to the final of Euro 2024, where they faced Spain. It was the first time in England's history they'd made back-to-back Euros finals! Kane and Bellingham both started, and Bellingham's delicate assist for Cole Palmer gave England hope – only for them to concede late on and lose 2–1. ■

WHAT THE DOUBTERS SAY

"More failure! Those 'GOATs' can't have contributed much to their country."

WRONG!

With two major finals, one semi-final and one quarter-final in their last four tournaments, Kane and Bellingham's England team is one of the most successful of all time (especially compared to the Golden Generation!)

And yes, before someone points it out, England won the World Cup in 1966, but remember, they only made the quarter-finals of the next World Cup in 1970. Then they didn't even qualify for the two after that!

So let's sum up Kane's contribution to that success:

- The first man to captain England in four major tournaments
- England's all-time record goalscorer
- Golden Boot winner at the 2018 World Cup and joint top scorer at Euro 2024

- The most ever competitive appearances (89) for England
- Most appearances at major tournaments (29) in England history
- Most goals at major tournaments (15) in England history
- 9 goals in 15 knockout games

And now Bellingham's contribution to that success:

- The youngest England player to ever feature at a major tournament
- The first 17-year-old to play a full match for England since 1881
- A member of England's leadership group before the age of 21
- The second England player to score at the World Cup and Euros before the age of 21 (after Ballon d'Or winner Michael Owen)
- Scorer of a brilliant bicycle kick against Slovakia to give England one of their most iconic moments in recent history
- A delicate assist for Cole Palmer in the final of Euro 2024

While the record-breaking, country-changing Kane may be coming towards the end of his England career, he's still got plenty of chances for international success. After all, didn't a 35-year-old Lionel Messi win a World Cup when he was considered "past it"?

And Bellingham has already achieved so much for his country. In his first four years as an England player, the young icon reached two major finals and one quarter-final. He's proved that he's a talisman for the Three Lions, a superstar who fans can pin their hopes and dreams on. Imagine what he might be able to achieve in his next four years!

WHO'S THE WINNER?

Captain Fantastic. England's all-time record scorer. National legend. While Kane is the clear winner when it comes to country contribution, he has time on his side. Bellingham has a long way to go to contribute even more than Kane has. We're so excited for what's to come…

But out of these two, who has contributed the most to the game?

THE GAME

Football is constantly changing, both on the pitch and off the pitch. Though it's still too early to judge our GOATs' overall contribution to the game, they've already helped to change the sport we all know and love. So, let's see how they've made a difference.

HARRY KANE

We've already learned how Kane has rewritten the forward role, inspiring José Mourinho to say, "Maybe he will be responsible for everyone that loves football to change the way people look at a striker. A striker can be the man of the match without scoring."

And we've also learned how Kane's late arrival on the big stage showed that talent can take time to develop.

But now we're going to focus on Kane using his status to make a difference…

Making a Stand by Taking a Knee

ENGLAND 1 | 0 CROATIA

13 JUNE 2021 • WEMBLEY STADIUM

The eyes of Europe were on England as they walked out for their opening Euro 2020 match, led by captain Harry Kane. Would they make a stand against racism by taking the knee before kick-off?

Taking the knee was started by American footballer Colin Kaepernick in 2016. When the national anthem played before his matches, he would kneel. Kaepernick's gesture was meant as a peaceful protest against racism. Soon, lots of other stars in different sports were also taking the knee before games … including the England football team.

But not everybody was happy with the anti-racism gesture. Some fans claimed that footballers shouldn't be political.

So what did Kane and his team do before their big match? They all knelt down in a powerful statement against racism.

From the crowd, there were boos … but those boos were soon drowned out by cheers and applause!

"Education is the biggest thing we can do," Kane later said when asked if his team would continue to take the knee. "We have all … seen teammates and friends racially abused, so we want to help make a change." ■

When Kane speaks, people listen. At the 2022 World Cup, England carried on taking the knee.

Racism still exists, but Kane continues to speak out in the hope that his team can fight against inequality on and off the pitch.

JUDE BELLINGHAM

Football has never been busier. Tournaments are expanding, new European competitions are being created, and teams are flying off on bigger pre-season tours. The demands on players have never been greater. Increasingly, the best ability that a player can have is their availability.

No player represents this more than Jude Bellingham…

MORE, MORE, MORE!

BELLINGHAM BEATS THE CLOCK

ENGLAND 0 | 0 SLOVENIA

25 JUNE 2024
RHEINENERGIESTADION, COLOGNE

When the referee blew for full-time, England's players couldn't hide their disappointment – particularly Bellingham! For 90 minutes, England's attacking midfielder could find no way through Slovenia's packed defence. It may not have been his greatest performance, but the Euro 2024 game represented an incredible achievement: it was Bellingham's 251st competitive senior game before turning 21.

Yes, Bellingham had now played a total of 16,001 minutes at the highest level of domestic and international football before turning 21 (18,944 minutes including his time with League One Birmingham).

Just two players in modern history had managed more minutes at the top level before they turned 21: midfielder Cesc Fàbregas (16,691 minutes) and goalkeeper Gianluigi Donnarumma (18,309 minutes).

But there was no time to dwell on his achievement. There was yet another game to come five days later, the day after his 21st birthday – and Bellingham would have to be at his best.

So how did he celebrate? With that incredible last-minute single kick against Slovakia that helped to send England through to the next round! What ability … and what availability! ■

WHO'S THE WINNER?

The evolved forward versus the minute-hungry midfielder. The voice for equality versus the wonderkid. They've both made a difference to the game we love … and they'll carry on doing so until they're retired (and beyond!). Once again, Kane has time on his side, but don't write off Bellingham just yet…

SO COME ON THEN… WHO IS THE CONTRIBUTION GOAT?

In this Contribution section, we've looked at the impact Kane and Bellingham have had on club, country and the game of football itself. Now it's time to put those arguments into action and VOTE FOR THE GOAT!

We're going with age before Bellingham, so over to Seth to argue for Kane.

SETH'S CASE FOR KANE

Developing at Borussia Dortmund and then dominating at Madrid sounds easy, right? Let's be honest: even Matt could play in Real Madrid's team and look half decent.

But do you know what isn't easy? Taking the Harry Kane option. Spending your golden years at a Tottenham Hotspur team with no history of success and little money to strengthen their ambitions. Yet this homegrown hero took Spurs to new heights, securing their best finish for 50 years and taking them to within a whisker of Champions League glory.

He became Tottenham Hotspur's all-time record goalscorer and one of the greatest players in their history.

And he became England's all-time men's record goalscorer and one of the greatest players in their history, leading them to back-to-back finals in the Euros for the first time ever.

Give Harry Kane the career of Jude Bellingham and he'd win just as much, maybe even more.

But stick Jude Bellingham into Harry Kane's Tottenham Hotspur team, or that England side who'd just lost to Iceland, and he wouldn't contribute half as much as Harry has.

When it comes to club and country, Kane is the Contribution King. Case closed.

MATT'S CASE FOR BELLINGHAM

Yes, Jude Bellingham now plays for the mighty Real Madrid, but he still had to work his way up to the top like everyone else. And how did he do that? By shining the brightest, season after season, for team after team!

In his one year at Birmingham City, Bellingham made such a big impact that they retired his shirt.

In his three years at Borussia Dortmund, he won the German Cup and he would surely have lifted the league title too if he hadn't got injured.

In his first year at Real Madrid, he helped them win three trophies!

Plus, in his five years as a senior international,

Jude has also already helped England reach two Euro finals and a World Cup quarter-final.

So, not a bad contribution, considering he's still in his early 20s! And just think what more Bellingham will have achieved by the time he's as old as Harry Kane...

Matt
I'm hearing lots of words from you, but I'm not seeing many trophies from Kane. What a great contribution he's made... NOT!

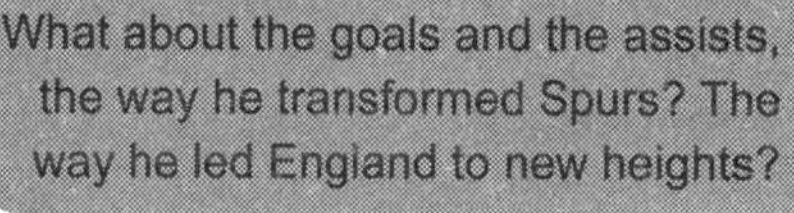

Matt
Oh yes, all those ways he won trophies. I've had a *brilliant* time celebrating England's runner-up medals.

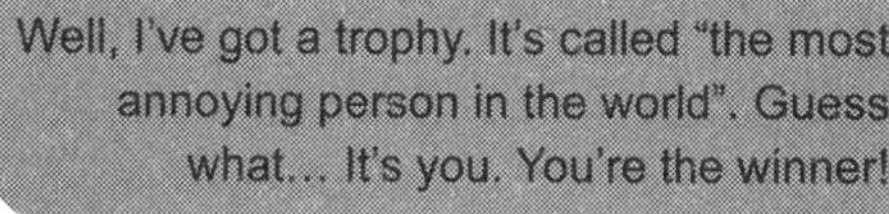

Matt
Sounds as if I'm just like Jude: a born winner...

THE SCORES ARE IN:

	KANE	BELLINGHAM
CLUB CONTRIBUTION	9/10	10/10
COUNTRY CONTRIBUTION	9/10	7/10
GAME CONTRIBUTION	7/10	7/10
TOTAL SCORE	25/30	24/30

So those are our opinions, whether you wanted to hear them or not! But are we right? Who do you think is the Contribution GOAT – Kane or Bellingham?

My Contribution GOAT is

....

EXTRA TIME

Let's make this as short and sweet as a Bellingham "Who else?" celebration. We're walking to the changing rooms. We've made our points, explained our reasons and given heaps of evidence. Let's quickly remind ourselves of our key points…

CHARACTER

Kane

He's loyal, dedicated and composed.

Doubt him at your peril – Kane has remarkable resilience.

Captain Kane leads England with composure and consistency.

Bellingham

He's confident, driven and mature.

This big-game baller is the Prince of Pressure.

He's a natural leader who inspires with his words and actions.

SKILLS

Kane

He's quicker and stronger than you think!

A world-class finisher and passer.

This intelligent and adaptable striker forms deadly duos.

Bellingham

This all-action player is a physical warrior.

A master of all trades.

4+8+9+10… Where can't this number 31 play on a pitch?!

STATS

Kane
This goalscorer is a goal machine!

His trophy cabinet is filled with Golden Boot awards.

It took a long time, but in 2025 he claimed his first-ever team trophy!

Bellingham
His all-round game can't just be measured in goals and assists.

He's already won the Bundesliga and La Liga Player of the Year awards.

He's won lots of team trophies, including a treble in one season!

CONTRIBUTION

Kane
He's Mr Tottenham, who's "one of our own".

Tottenham Hotspur and England's all-time record scorer who led his country to back-to-back Euro finals.

He speaks up to help those around him.

Bellingham
One retired shirt, lots of trophies. He's succeeded at every club he's played for.

He gave us THAT moment against Slovakia – a key player for his country already.

His availability is as good as his ability, allowing him to clock up minutes.

OUR RATINGS

	CATEGORY	KANE	BELLINGHAM
CHARACTER	PERSONALITY RATING	8/10	8/10
	MINDSET RATING	9/10	9/10
	LEADERSHIP RATING	9/10	8/10
SKILLS	PHYSICAL SKILLS	7/10	9/10
	TECHNICAL SKILLS	10/10	9/10
	TACTICAL SKILLS	10/10	10/10
STATS	PERFORMANCE STATS RATING	9/10	8/10
	INDIVIDUAL ACHIEVEMENTS RATING	8/10	9/10
	TEAM STATS RATING	7/10	9/10
CONTRIBUTION	CLUB CONTRIBUTION	9/10	10/10
	COUNTRY CONTRIBUTION	9/10	7/10
	GAME CONTRIBUTION	7/10	7/10
	TOTAL RATING	102/120	103/120

OUR ENGLAND GOAT IS ...

BELLINGHAM!

It's been an epic England battle and this is how our scores have added up. There's only a point in it, but Bellingham takes the crown. And although we've argued a lot, there's one thing we agree on. These talented two could really have England's fans singing with joy in the near future.

Seth
It's coming home, it's coming—

Matt
Your singing is about as charismatic as Kane in a press conference.

Seth
Hey, first of all, you're wrong. Second, we're supposed to have finished arguing now.

Matt
But I like arguing!

Seth
So do I. Fine, I'll stop singing, but we need to show the reader our GOATs' highlights.

Matt
You mean like a *Match of the Day* for this book?

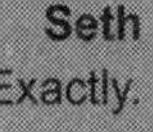

Seth
Exactly.

Matt
And how does that theme tune go?

Before we hand over to you to make your final GOAT decision, there are two final things to consider.

From dream debuts to great goals and crazy knockout matches, Kane and Bellingham have packed their careers with top moments. We've chosen what we think are the five best for you to enjoy.

Finally you need to hear what the world of football thinks of our England GOATs. After that, it will be time for you to choose your GOAT.

KANE'S TOP MOMENTS

DERBY DELIGHT

TOTTENHAM HOTSPUR 2 | 1 ARSENAL

7 FEBRUARY 2015 • PREMIER LEAGUE

How to announce yourself in your first-ever North London derby? Score both goals in a 2–1 victory! Kane's winner came at 86 minutes, sending Spurs fans into wild celebrations. ■

THE FIRST GOLDEN BOOT

2015–16 SEASON • PREMIER LEAGUE

After failing to score in his first six games of the 2015–16 season, critics suggested Kane was just a "one-season wonder". How wrong they were. Kane's 25 goals won him the Premier League's Golden Boot! ■

OFF TO THE FINAL

ENGLAND 2 | 1 DENMARK

7 JULY 2021 • EURO 2020 SEMI-FINAL

Fans couldn't believe it when Kane missed his 104th minute penalty! But never mind, the rebound came straight back to Kane, who hit it in to send England to their first major final since 1966. ■

CAPTAIN FANTASTIC, RECORD-BREAKER!

ITALY 1 | 2 ENGLAND

23 MARCH 2023 • EURO 2024 QUALIFIERS

Kane made no mistake from the penalty spot this time as his 44th-minute strike beat Italy keeper Gianluigi Donnarumma, to make Kane the England men's all-time record scorer. ■

FINALLY, A TROPHY

BAYERN MUNICH 2 | 0 BORUSSIA MÖNCHENGLADBACH

10 MAY 2025 • BUNDESLIGA

It was the moment Kane had been waiting for his whole career: his first trophy! Bayern Munich had already won the Bundesliga but had to wait to be handed the title after this final match. Kane celebrated in the best way possible: Michael Olise's cross was perfect, allowing Kane to nod home for his 25th Bundesliga goal of the season. When the whistle blew, Kane finally lifted the trophy! ■

BELLINGHAM'S TOP MOMENTS

HEY JUDE! A NAME TO REMEMBER

BIRMINGHAM CITY 2 | 1 STOKE CITY

31 AUGUST 2019 • EFL CHAMPIONSHIP

Birmingham City's wonderkid came off the bench to net the winner for his beloved Blues on his home debut. "It's something I've dreamed of since I was a boy," he said after the game. ■

THE FIRST OF MANY

BORUSSIA DORTMUND 4 | 1 RB LEIPZIG

13 MAY 2021 • GERMAN CUP FINAL

Bellingham hit the big time with his first-ever trophy win. Starting in central midfield, he was everywhere as Borussia Dortmund raced into a 3–0 lead before half-time! The move to Germany had paid off. ■

WELCOME TO EL CLÁSICO, JUDE

BARCELONA 1 | 2 REAL MADRID

28 OCTOBER 2023 • LA LIGA

In his first El Clásico, Bellingham smashed home an equalizer in the 68th minute from 30 yards before bundling home a stoppage-time winner. ■

INCREDI-BELL

ENGLAND 2 | 1 SLOVAKIA

30 JUNE 2024
EUROPEAN CHAMPIONSHIPS
ROUND OF 16

With his team losing 1–0 in the 95th minute, up jumped Jude – who else? – to equalize with a heroic overhead kick! Bellingham had saved England from an embarrassing Euros exit, while giving the fans a moment they'll never forget. ■

CHAMPION OF CHAMPIONS

BORUSSIA DORTMUND 0 | 2 REAL MADRID

1 JUNE 2024 • CHAMPIONS LEAGUE FINAL

Bellingham's dream debut season at Real Madrid had the perfect ending … a Champions League final against former club Borussia Dortmund! Jude put in an all-action display, even assisting Vinícius Júnior's winner. ■

THE WORLD OF FOOTBALL DECIDES

It isn't just us who disagree about the England football GOAT. To help you make your final decision, we thought you might like a little help from some famous footballers and managers.

TEAM KANE

"I think Harry Kane is an incredible player. The goals he's scored, the assists and as of the last few years, I would say he's England's greatest-ever player."

WAYNE ROONEY, FORMER ENGLAND CAPTAIN

"When you think of Premier League greats, Kane is one of the best we've seen."

JAMIE CARRAGHER, PUNDIT AND FORMER ENGLAND PLAYER

"He's one of the best players in the world."

JAMAL MUSIALA, BAYERN MUNICH PLAYER

"Look at the number 9s around the world – Messi and Ronaldo are different players – and I can't see a better one."

GARETH SOUTHGATE, FORMER ENGLAND MANAGER

"He is a complete player."

ZINEDINE ZIDANE, FORMER REAL MADRID PLAYER AND MANAGER

"He is a GOAT in this league, in this sport. He is a great example."

CRISTIAN STELLINI, FORMER TOTTENHAM HOTSPUR ASSISTANT COACH

"Harry Kane remains one of the best strikers I have ever seen in my life."

PEP GUARDIOLA, MANCHESTER CITY MANAGER

TEAM BELLINGHAM

"He's one of the most gifted players I've ever seen. I don't see a weakness in his game. I think he will be the best midfielder in the world."

PHIL FODEN, MANCHESTER CITY AND ENGLAND PLAYER

"He's a top boy with extraordinary talent."

LUKA MODRIĆ, REAL MADRID AND CROATIA PLAYER

"Decision-making. End product. Final pass. The kid has everything."

ROY KEANE, PUNDIT AND FORMER MANCHESTER UNITED PLAYER

"He looks like he can do absolutely everything."

GARY NEVILLE, PUNDIT AND FORMER ENGLAND PLAYER

"Jude is in the bracket we love – high-performance, low-maintenance."

GARETH SOUTHGATE, FORMER ENGLAND MANAGER

"I think he is a future England captain."

WAYNE ROONEY, FORMER ENGLAND CAPTAIN

"I think Jude Bellingham for his age and what he's accomplished so far in his short career, he's better than anything we've seen."

PAUL SCHOLES, PUNDIT AND FORMER ENGLAND FOOTBALLER

IN THE WORDS OF OTHER GOATS

"I think he is an excellent player."

PELÉ ON KANE

"Wow, what a goalscorer!"

DIEGO MARADONA ON KANE

"Playing with Jude is incredible. It's a pleasure every single time."

KYLIAN MBAPPÉ ON BELLINGHAM

"He will give a lot to Madrid, because the boy, I think he will be extraordinary."

CRISTIANO RONALDO ON BELLINGHAM

IN THEIR OWN WORDS

"He's a brilliant player, he's full of confidence at the moment and has amazing ability ... he is going to be the future of our team."

KANE ON BELLINGHAM

"He's a world-class player, my captain for the national team, and I love him as a player and as a person."

BELLINGHAM ON KANE

PEEP! That's all, football fans! We've travelled through the careers of Harry Kane and Jude Bellingham, sharing their many highs and their occasional lows (but as we know, these two ALWAYS bounce back). Along the way, we've learned all about their …

- Characters
- Skills
- Stats
- Contributions.

And now it's time for you to decide. Yes, these guys are great, but which one is the greatest? Who is going to bring it home? Will you be kissing your ring finger in celebration like Kane or screaming "Who else?" like Jude. It all comes down to you…

My England GOAT is

……………………………………

Matt Oldfield grew up in Southampton, playing football with his brother Tom. The two brothers are the authors of the bestselling Ultimate Football Heroes series – fun football biographies that tell the exciting life stories of superstars from the playground through to the pitch. He is also the author of *Johnny Ball: Accidental Football Genius* and *Unbelievable Football*, which won the *Telegraph* Children's Sports Book of the Year in 2020. He has also written books on cricket and rugby.

Seth Burkett is a former professional footballer and futsal player. Having played professional football in Brazil for Sorriso EC and in Sri Lanka, Seth now dedicates his time to writing and speaking in schools. He is the co-author of *Play Like Your Football Heroes* with Matt Oldfield.